Tony Shead has published one novel, *Travelling Hopefully*, and a previous volume of short stories, *After the Iceberg*, with Book Guild Publishing.

DEATH IN THE ROUGH
AND OTHER STORIES

Tony Shead

Book Guild Publishing
Sussex, England

First published in Great Britain in 2006 by
The Book Guild Ltd
25 High Street
Lewes, East Sussex
BN7 2LU

Typesetting in Baskerville by
Keyboard Services, Luton, Bedfordshire

Printed in Great Britain by
Athenaeum Press Ltd, Gateshead

A catalogue record for this book is available from
The British Library

ISBN 1 84624 052 2

Contents

Rainy Days

Film star Robert Sheldon's career was at a halt. He had become rich and famous through having been selected eight years previously to play d'Artagnan in a film involving 'The Three Musketeers'. No more minor roles in minor films and plays: the immediate success of the first production had led to six more films about the musketeers' adventures, each one accruing vast sums at the box office. After the third film he changed his agent and arranged a new deal for himself, to include, for the first time, a share in gross profits. Along the way he divorced his first wife and married another, who then divorced him. He was now sitting in a villa he had rented near Grasse in the South of France, looking out at the heavy rain outside.

In fact, he had been doing a bit too much sitting inside and watching rain, he thought. He was half-way through a three month let starting 1st June and most days the weather had been wet and windy. None of his various guests had so far

1

stayed long, unsettled by continuing gloomy forecasts and irritated by the wonderful summer being experienced in England. And this holiday was meant to have been such fun, with work out of the way and a chance to relish his money and achievements. True, his contract hadn't been renewed, although the producers were still making the 'musketeer' films, but at fifty he was thought to have become too lined in the face and too heavy to go on playing the lead. There was an absence of any other offers – the later character and cameo parts and the knighthood were yet to come – so he had all the time he needed to enjoy himself, deliberately banishing the future from his mind.

This afternoon, rain or no rain, he would go into Cannes. Latterly, with no guests on the immediate horizon and on his own, his sorties had become restricted to shopping in the small village nearby and visiting the market in Grasse. The idea had been for his girlfriend in England to spend the whole holiday with him, but then she was offered a part in a Noel Coward play to tour the provinces, and that was the end of that. He was seeing no one apart from Marie, the woman who came daily to clean and occasionally cook for him.

He motored down the long winding road to the coast. He parked the car in the covered car-park near the sea. When he came out he walked along the *Croisette* towards the big hotels. He was making his way to the terrace of the Carlton Hotel when a young girl came up to him. Smiling, she said to him in English: 'I've enjoyed your films so much.'

There was a time when these sudden and unwanted approaches caused him considerable annoyance. Usually he gave a weak grin and hurried by. But something struck him about this girl. He noticed how strangely thin she was, and young, probably no more than seventeen, with a fragile, barely formed figure. He looked at her smooth, white face, gazing at him through blue eyes.

The sun had come out – was this to be a change in the weather? – and as he studied her, in her shabby denim shorts and worn-looking shirt, people bustled by under a clearing sky.

'Thank you, very kind,' he murmured, adding inconsequentially: 'I think I'll go and lie on the beach, now we've got a bit of sun.'

'I'll show you a good place,' she answered.

He did not protest, and together they walked to a roped-off area the other side of the road from a line of shops. The beach boy seemed to know her and laid out two mattresses by an opened parasol.

'He lets me sleep here at nights in his shed,' the girl remarked.

'Have you no money then?'

'I've spent what little I came here with. My boyfriend was meant to be following me out from

England. I go every day to the rendezvous we arranged but he's not there.'

'So what will you do?'

'Carry on waiting for him, I suppose.'

Pulling himself together, Robert decided to move on. He wished he had not got into conversation in the first place. Some girl trying to pick him up. She would probably be asking him for money soon. Nevertheless he pulled some notes out of the pocket of his shorts. 'Here, have this,' he said, 'at least you'll be able to eat for a few days.' The girl took the money silently and did not look at him as he walked away.

Robert bought a paper and sat in the sun on the Carlton Hotel terrace. After a second cup of coffee, he decided to go for a walk along the *Croisette*, and his spirits rose at the sight of a party of beautiful, scantily clad girls walking along amongst the crowd of everyday holiday-makers. He resolved to make better use of his time and over the next few days visited Biot, Mougins and all the ancient villages and places of interest in his locality. At Mougins one afternoon he bought a large brightly coloured landscape painting. He was returning with it when he was met by an agitated Marie, to his surprise still at the house, although it was hours past her normal working time. 'A girl's come to see you,' she blurted out, disapprovingly. 'She won't go away and I wasn't

4

going to leave her here with no one to see what she was up to. Says she knows you.'

Robert went out into the garden – Marie explained she was not letting the girl into the house – and he recognised the person he had met the week before in Cannes, hair untidy and in the same shabby clothes.

'How did you find my address?' he asked sharply.

'The local paper said you had rented a villa near Roquefort-les-Pins, so I came up here and asked in the village where your house was.'

Incensed, Robert said, 'If you have no money, how did you get here?'

She had hitchhiked part of the way and then walked along the side of the road, finally walking to the house from the village. Robert reckoned the journey must have taken her several hours.

'Can I sit down somewhere?' she asked meekly, 'and perhaps have a glass of water?'

Thawing slightly, Robert led her to the terrace. 'What do you want of me? You'll be lucky if I don't call the police.'

He told Marie the girl was some misguided fan and that he could take care of the matter.

When Marie came the next day, she was surprised to find the girl still there. Robert had decided to let her stay the night, on the understanding that she left – even if he had to hire a taxi to take her back to Cannes – the following morning.

There was little of value for her to steal and how would she transport it? He felt sorry for her and she looked in need of a decent meal and a good night's sleep. She helped him prepare a cold supper, which they ate on the terrace. Shortly after, he led her to a bedroom and showed her where she could have a shower.

According to her story, forced out of her over supper, she had quarrelled with her mother back in England and run off to Cannes. She was planning to elope with her boyfriend, but had ended up on her own. Her friend had been detained at Heathrow airport. Why? She didn't know. He'd told her it was nothing serious and to wait for him. She'd watched as he was led away by airport police from the final departure lounge. Lying in his bed, Robert was thinking about this strange story early the next morning, when he heard the door open. Clad in a robe from the bedroom, he saw the girl come silently towards him.

'Are you awake?' she whispered, and without waiting for an answer, sat down at the foot of the bed. 'The house was so quiet and I was frightened. I just had to make sure you were here.'

The sooner I send this girl on her way, the better, thought Robert.

Over cups of coffee in the kitchen a little while later, the girl told him her name was Greta. 'I wasn't completely honest with you last night,' she said. 'I knew the police were looking for my boyfriend. They suspect him of being a terrorist.'

'And would they be right?'

'He has always denied it to me. But he often disappears for days on end, when he's meant to be studying in London. He's half Egyptian and half French. I think his parents live in Paris.'

After a pause, Robert said with a smile, 'Perhaps he chose this part of France for your supposed elopement to make an agreed contact?'

Ignoring or not noticing any sarcasm, Greta replied, 'You remember I told you I was going every day to a rendezvous I'd agreed with my boyfriend in case of trouble? Well, I often saw a funny-looking man there, who might also have been waiting.'

'How was he funny-looking?'

'Very swarthy with long black hair. Looked an Arab. I saw he had begun to notice me and one day he followed me until I gave him the slip. I got frightened – I am sure there is some connection and I wanted to get away. That is the reason I came up here. I had nowhere else to go.'

'So I suppose you'd like me to buy you a ticket and send you back to England?'

'I'd pay you back, I promise, once I got home.'

Greta duly left in the taxi Robert had had in mind earlier, but it was to Nice airport and with money in her pocket to buy a ticket to London. A phone call had told him that there were currently no available seats on any flights to London, but he sent her off nonetheless, telling her to wait – camp out overnight if necessary – until an airline could take her. She was probably telling him a pack of lies, but if it *were* true, it was a situation he wanted to steer well clear of, and at the price of an air ticket, it was cheap.

He was therefore extremely irritated when early that evening the doorbell rang and he saw the girl standing outside. She had not been able to buy a ticket to London as all the flights were still full, she said, and had been sitting in a café in the arrivals area, when she noticed the man she had described to him standing in the crowd and evidently waiting to meet someone off a plane. Then her boyfriend had appeared and the two men grasped each other and started talking animatedly.

They made their way to the café and before she had time to move they both spotted her. As she got to her feet, they grabbed her. The man she called the Arab seemed to know exactly who she was and said urgently to her boyfriend that she must be kept out of the way for a few days. When the boyfriend said 'how?' and 'where?', the other man just smiled. She started appealing to the boyfriend, said all she wanted was to get back home, but he shook his head, saying there was too much at stake.

They had been talking in the hall, but moved into the living-room and Robert poured out some white wine for them both. Sitting down, Greta informed Robert she was now convinced the boy-friend did not love her, had probably only arranged the flight out together as a cover for himself.

Robert did not know whether to believe her story or not. When he could get a word in, he said, 'One thing you haven't explained: how did you get away from them and could they have followed you?'

They both gave a start as the quiet of the evening was shattered by the ring of the doorbell. Getting to his feet, Robert said, 'You'd better hide somewhere. Leave this to me.'

He opened the door cautiously. It was the local *gendarme*, leaning on his bicycle. He knew the man by sight from his visits to the village.

'Sorry to trouble you, *monsieur*,' the visitor began, speaking slowly in French, 'but evidently there's a bit of a panic going on down on the coast about a possible terrorist attack and they're seeking two men and a young girl. All the local stations have been contacted to see if they can help. I've been talking to several people in the village and your *femme de ménage*, Marie, mentioned she had seen a girl corresponding to the police description visiting you in your house. I'm probably bothering you unnecessarily,' he added apologetically.

'I know the girl, she's English. I can vouch for

her,' Robert heard himself say. 'She's no longer here and I don't know where she's gone.'

"I'm sorry to have disturbed you,' the policeman said, touching his cap and wishing him a good night.

Greta appeared in the hall as he was shutting the door. 'That was the local *gendarme*,' Robert told her, 'helping to look for what sounds like the three of you.'

'I'll tell you how I got away,' she said. 'The three of us were still standing by the café table when two policemen appeared from nowhere. I ran out into the crowd. I assumed the policemen had detained them – the policemen couldn't run after me as well.'

'Well, somehow or other your two friends seem to be still on the loose. I think you'll have to go down to the police station at Cannes and tell them all you know. I expect you're the young girl they're also looking for.'

'Well, if I am, it's only because the policemen saw me with them. I know nothing and can tell them nothing, bar giving descriptions of the other two, which they already have. But if you insist, can I stay the night if I promise to go to the police in the morning? I won't mention I was here, of course.'

Robert knew he was playing with fire, but felt he had little alternative. He'd have to get her out early, before Marie came. After supper, they were watching the television news. The main story was a suspected terrorist attack on one of the large hotels along the *Croisette* at Cannes. There were pictures of a cordoned-off, deserted promenade with no parked cars anywhere. Police were surrounding the three main hotels.

Shaken, Greta remarked, 'I don't quite see how those two men on their own could do anything serious.'

'Leave a nice bomb in a suitcase somewhere?' queried Robert. 'Or maybe they were meeting up with accomplices and planning to park a car stuffed with explosives. The police have obviously had a tip-off. Incidentally, I've been wondering how your friend got himself released after his arrest at Heathrow airport. Maybe the powers-that-be took a chance on his leading them to something down here.'

There was no sign of Greta when Robert rose at six o'clock the following morning. Turning on the radio, he heard that four men had been arrested in connection with the feared attack and the search had been called off. He went to Greta's room to tell her the news, but she wasn't there. Going into the living-room, he looked out and saw her splashing in the swimming-pool. Quickly he returned to her room. He found the little leather bag she carried with her and which

11

appeared to be her only luggage. A spare shirt, some pants, wash things … and underneath at the bottom some euros and her passport. He took out the passport. Her Christian name was Greta all right with a German-sounding surname. Her age, considerably older than he had supposed, twenty six.

He went into the sitting-room hurriedly to see her emerging naked from the pool.

'I thought I'd go and have a swim before I left,' she announced, smiling. 'I'll just go and grab a towel.'

Robert made some coffee and when she appeared told her what he had heard on the news.

'I think we'll accept the fact the hunt is off,' he said, 'and I'll drive you straight to the airport. You'll just have to hope they're not still looking for you.'

He knew Air France had an eleven o'clock flight, and on telephoning, was told there were seats available.

'Can I have some more money please?' asked Greta. 'I made a bit of a hole in what you gave me for the ticket, getting that taxi to bring me back here.'

On the way down to the coast in his car, Robert was feeling a sense of relief that he was, hopefully, at last getting the girl off his hands. Her stories might be true, or they might not; all he knew was that he wanted to be rid of her. He parked right outside the airport entrance and helped her out. He was holding out his hand to say goodbye, when she tiptoed up and kissed him firmly on the mouth. A traffic controller was already signalling to him to move on. As he got back into the driving seat, he caught a final glimpse of her scurrying into the building.

In case of trouble, he had no intention of being seen with her inside, but at the same time he intended to make sure that she caught the plane. He parked the car in one of the airport parking areas and, turning on the radio, sat and waited. He reckoned that, assuming the plane was leaving on time, she would have to be in the final departure area within an hour, and it would be safe for him to go and make enquiries.

It was a quiet period and he went up to one of the only two Air France reception desks being serviced. The two girls, in their neat uniforms and with carefully coiffed hair, were chatting to each other and laughing.

'I wanted to check whether a certain lady caught the eleven o'clock London plane all right,' he enquired pleasantly, giving Greta's surname.

The girl whom he had addressed started tapping at a machine and then stared at her screen.

'No reservation by anybody of that name on that flight, sir,' she replied.

Her friend was listening to the conversation and asked the first girl to repeat the passenger's name. Robert heard her whisper across in French, 'I've just checked her into the flight to Algiers.'

'Where do you say she was going?' he asked politely.

'I'm afraid we're not allowed to divulge that information, sir,' the first girl said. But he had heard enough.

When Robert got outside, it had started raining. Feeling distinctly uneasy, he began planning an early return to England.

Flight from Anguilla

William Forwood was sitting on his own in the bar at Antigua airport one April afternoon, when he learnt that he would have to wait several hours for the badly delayed plane that serviced the outer islands. He walked over to the stand of a local company he had noticed in the arrivals hall and chartered a light aircraft to take him on to Anguilla. It had been a long flight from London and he was tired.

Presently a tall, attractive blonde girl in a sky-blue suit and cap approached him. She put his case on a trolley and, with a smiling instruction to follow her, marched him out of the back of the building. They walked round the tarmac, eventually stopping at a far corner. She lifted his case into the hold of a small four-seater plane. William looked around for the pilot, as he proceeded to strap himself into the front seat. The girl was now talking to a uniformed man, who had come towards them.

Throwing out a final remark and with a wave

15

of her hand, to his surprise it was she who then swung herself into the pilot's seat. Removing her cap, she thrust it under a gold epaulette. Then, turning to face her passenger, she announced that seatbelts should be kept fastened throughout the flight, the weather was expected to remain clear, flight time was one hour. She started the engine, checking and re-checking the controls. Then, with an ear-splitting roar, they were down the runway and into the sky.

'What brings you to Anguilla?' the pilot asked him, as the plane settled on its course.

'I don't know if you've ever heard of the late Lord Canningstoke,' William replied. 'I believe he and his wife used to come to the island quite often at one time, before he got too ill to travel. The wife's heard about an old plantation that might be for sale, which she wants me to look at. Wonderful situation evidently, but I gather the estate house needs a bit of attention. I'm to tell her if I think anything can be done with it. If so, cost no object and she could end up with a nice holiday house.'

The girl did not pursue the conversation, so he contented himself staring down at the sun-spattered blue and green sea. Small islands were coming into sight under a cloudless sky. At one moment his companion pointed to a larger island on the port side and shouted out its name.

When they eventually arrived at Anguilla, the airport's landing and berthing area was deserted,

16

bar a few light planes parked in a row along the side of the main building. William and the pilot had become quite friendly, talking and laughing together in the latter part of the journey, and now the girl – who had introduced herself as Carmen – was retrieving his case from the hold and pointing to where he should enter the airport building. Smiling, she shook hands. Walking slowly towards where he had been directed, he watched over his shoulder as she got back into the plane and taxied towards where the other light aircraft were standing

'Quite a girl!' thought William.

Once inside, he followed a sign saying 'Passport Control'. A dark-skinned official looked at him suspiciously as he fumbled for his passport. He was then told to fill in a form. On returning to the official's booth, William was rewarded with the sound of loud rubber stamping and the passport and the form were handed back to him. The official gestured towards an area marked 'Customs and Immigration'.

When he reached the customs, there was not a soul in attendance behind the long luggage-inspection counters. Had they had all gone off duty for the day? He was considering what to do when a deep English voice hailed him from behind. Turning, he saw a burly European of some sixty years of age standing before him, right hand outstretched.

'The name's Conway,' the stranger said. 'Couldn't help but see you from where I'm sitting over there.' He motioned towards a gloomy corner, which William now noticed contained several tables and chairs. 'I'm in the same spot as you, but you've got to wait for them to reappear. You can't just walk out of the building.'

'Where have *they* gone to?' countered William.

'Well, there are only two of them and at this time of day they always go off to have their tea!'

William was puzzling over this information when two native customs officers suddenly came into view on the other side of the long counter. Catching sight of William's companion, one of them called out, 'Hi, Mr Conway, what have you got for us to inspect?'

Mr Conway shuffled off to find his luggage and William plonked his case down on the table. He gave his passport and the stamped form to the officer who had spoken, loudly pronouncing the word 'tourist'. At the same time the officer's colleague, who was starting to make a telephone call, interrupted him with a query. The officer distractedly marked a sign in white chalk on William's case and motioned to him to go on through.

Now to find a taxi and get himself to the hotel in the northern part of the island, where he had booked a room. The sun was going down, but he suddenly found it insuperably hot. Taking off his jacket and putting it over his arm, he looked around for the taxi stand. There was a big enough sign, but no sign of any actual taxis. He was warding off the attentions of a dirty-looking individual with no vehicle anywhere in sight, eager to take him wherever he wanted, when Mr Conway emerged from the airport.

'Where d'you want to go, old boy?'

William told him.

'Very near where I'm off to,' Mr Conway continued. 'Walk over to the car-park with me and we can be on our way.'

Mr Conway's car was fairly ancient, and combined with the narrow, pot-holed roads, the journey took almost an hour. Mr Conway was a keen talker and there was soon little William did not know about him. He was a writer by profession, who owned a house on the island and was accustomed to spending a few months of every year there. He was currently in the middle of such a visit and was returning after a few days with friends in Antigua. William dutifully told him the reason for his own visit. Mr Conway gave a sharp reaction: he had not only known Lord Canningstoke in his lifetime, but claimed to know the property that William was coming to inspect.

When they finally arrived at William's hotel, Mr Conway insisted on coming to the desk with him to make sure everything was in order. Afterwards, they had a drink together on the lawn, during which time William's new friend suggested he should come over to his house the following evening for dinner. 'I may have some news for you about that plantation,' he said. William was pleased to accept the invitation; he had only been to Anguilla once in his life before and knew no one.

That previous visit had been some twenty five years earlier. He had established his fine art dealership in London's West End the year before and had gone to New York to bid for an important old master painting that was coming up for sale at auction. He had bought it for what he considered a reasonable price, and within days had received a handsome offer from a west coast museum. At the auction he had run into an American private collector, whom he knew slightly, who had invited him to stay at his villa in the West Indies – on an island called Anguilla, near Antigua, he explained – on the way back home. William had politely declined, pleading pressure of business, but when the deal with the museum went through a week later, he was sufficiently elated to ask if he could change his mind. He needed a holiday and here was a ready-made one! The American had already left for Anguilla, but his New York office supplied William with the phone number.

Now he was hoping to relive that earlier happy time in the sun. He had been toying with the idea of another visit when, at a dinner party in

London, Lady Canningstoke had mentioned the opportunity she had been presented with on the very same island. Of similar age, in their early fifties, they had known each other for some time, both socially and – in her husband's lifetime – as dealer to client. Seeing William's interest, Lady Canningstoke went on to tell him that she was currently not up to travelling herself and how she needed someone she could trust to give her a frank opinion. William liked the idea of a holiday with a purpose behind it ... and so it came about.

It was Lady Canningstoke who had recommended the hotel where he was staying, as not only being near the site but as one of the best in Anguilla. It turned out to be a large, sprawling building of two storeys, with flower-filled gardens leading down to the water's edge, situated on the leeward side of the island and in theory out of the wind.

William had been allotted a spacious bedroom on the first floor with far-reaching views. The next morning, after a peaceful sleep, he arranged for a self-drive hire car to be delivered, and, after obtaining suitable directions, motored himself over to the plantation. Going along the desolate coast road, he suddenly saw an old house, standing high up and overlooking the sea, and recognised it from the description he had been given by Lady Canningstoke. After a while, an elderly caretaker answered his ringing of the bell at the closed iron entrance gates.

Opening the gates a fraction, the caretaker took William's visiting card. 'Yes, I was told you might be coming. Come in,' he said.

William had been prepared for a long argument about being let in, and was surprised that the caretaker recognised his name. Who had warned him? The property was not officially on the market and there was no estate agent that Lady Canningstoke could have contacted. Perhaps she had rung up a local friend and asked him to warn the caretaker of the impending visit.

'I'll show you the grounds first,' the caretaker announced. 'Excuse me a moment while I get some transport.' He reappeared with an electric buggy and they set off up the hill towards the house. Half-way up they stopped and walked up to a ridge on the left side of the drive. Standing on the top, William had a perfect view of all the land on the near side of the house: several acres of cane, alongside neglected fields and tumble-down woods. Here and there he spotted barns and small, primitive dwellings.

Driving round the side of the house, they next came to rest on an overgrown stone terrace running the length of the building at the back. The land ahead of them was level for a good hundred yards and then fell sharply away to reveal cattle grazing and elsewhere sparse growing crops. In the distance there was more unattended land.

'Over a hundred acres,' the caretaker remarked

proudly. 'I expect you've got the feel of the estate now, or enough for a first visit. Let's look round the house.'

William agreed readily. They started trudging round the ground-floor reception rooms, oak-panelled, some partly furnished, but all dusty and dirty. Got potential, William thought, noticing the high quality wooden floors and the professional way in which the windows had been set on the inside. He was not impressed with the downstairs lavatories and basins and the fitments in the vast kitchen, all of which would need to be replaced. Upstairs, he liked the bedrooms, although the bathrooms would all need modernising.

He had seen all he wanted to see and was keen to leave. 'I'll probably be back in a few days,' he told the caretaker. He was driven down to the entrance gates and was off. He could give Lady Canningstoke his layman's overall impression – all he had been asked to do. She would have to hire professionals to report on the state of the building itself, strength of the electricity and adequacy of the water supply. What she would think of the rundown farming activities, he did not know.

He spent the afternoon lazing on the beach. He would telephone Lady Canningstoke the following day. When evening came, he dressed in a shirt and dark trousers and motored himself to Mr

Conway's house. It was not difficult to find. Mr Conway was on the doorstep to greet him.

It was an old house, but modernised and attractively decorated inside. A fire had been lit and he sat down beside it. His host went to pour out brandies and soda and then sat down opposite him. William told him about the morning's expedition. 'We'll talk about it after dinner, when the "help" has gone,' was Mr Conway's only comment.

Back in their chairs later, after an excellent dinner of freshly caught fish served by a large, smiling native woman, Mr Conway raised the subject again.

'I'm taking you into my confidence here,' he began, 'but there is another party interested in that property.'

William raised his eyebrows.

'The leading light is a lady I've known for a long time, who lives in St Martin. You've probably heard of the island – half French and half Dutch. She lives on the French side, the side nearest to us and only half an hour away by boat. At the moment she owns and runs a restaurant there, but is keen to have her own hotel.'

'But to buy the place and then convert it, fit it out to modern standards . . .' murmured William.

'Right, would cost a bomb. But it wouldn't stop there. She is planning to put in a swimming-pool and tennis courts, *and* she would build an annexe to provide more bedrooms.'

'So she wouldn't be doing it all by herself?'

'No, she's got powerful backers, including one very prominent man, who lives on this island. It would not be Anguilla's biggest hotel, but the most luxurious. Certainly the most expensive!' Mr Conway added with a laugh.

Conversation ceased as he rose from his chair to go to his drinks cabinet.

'By the way, my name's Harold,' he remarked. 'You won't have heard of me, as I don't write under my real name.'

'Mine's William,' William said, as Harold returned to where they were sitting.

There was a pause while they sipped their drinks. Then Harold said: 'Look, William, you seem a decent, straightforward bloke, and I want to be fair with you. I'm going over to see this lady in a couple of days' time and – if you like the idea of meeting her – I was thinking of asking her if I could bring you. I won't say anything about your interest in the plantation on the phone. My visit is purely social; you're a friend I'm asking if I can bring along and let's see how the conversation develops when we're all sitting down together.'

'Certainly can't do any harm,' said William. 'And anyway I'd enjoy meeting her and going to St Martin.'

William decided to defer his telephone conversation with Lady Canningstoke for the time being. When the day came for the visit, Harold picked him up early at the hotel and they drove on to the small harbour from where the ferry boats operated. It was a clear day and the island, just five miles west, was visible in the distance.

They disembarked at the busy town on the water's edge and walked up the narrow main street, stopping outside a colourful restaurant. They sat down at an outside table and ordered two coffees from a hovering waiter. Before long a tall, slim, good-looking woman of around fifty emerged from inside.

'Lovely to see you again,' she said, shaking hands with Harold. She gave William a bright smile as he was introduced. 'I'm in the middle of getting everything organised for lunch, but I've got a table for us put aside and if you come back in about an hour, I'll be all yours.'

'In that case we might as well have a little tour of the island,' said Harold.

They found a taxi and made their way to La Samanna, several miles higher up on the west coast. A beautiful, secluded hotel, set amidst gardens and white stucco buildings reminiscent of a Greek island village. They wandered round the public rooms before negotiating the multi-level sweep of walkways to the beach below. They sat out at a little beach bar, enjoying the sunshine and watching the calm, blue sea.

The driver took them back to the harbour town by a round-about route and after visiting a few shops, they walked back to the restaurant. The waiter who had been looking after them earlier showed them to a corner table inside.

William noticed the owner had changed clothes and was looking more relaxed when she came to join them. 'My name's Anne-Marie and I'm half English and half French,' she said to William, 'in case you were wondering.'

'What made you settle here and start a restaurant?' he asked with a smile.

'My mother's family came from here and I have always liked it. The *ambiance*, the easygoing way of living... But I have got bigger ambitions, I want to own a hotel.'

'On St Martin?'

'No, I have got my eye on some land on another island.'

A waiter's arrival to take their orders precluded further conversation.

Much later, while they were all having coffee, Harold returned to the subject of Anne-Marie's future plans. She was quite frank, explaining how she had found an old plantation on Anguilla, which, properly converted, would be ideal. 'I realised I would need rich, influential partners, of course, and I think I have been lucky enough to find them,' she went on. 'Harold knows all about it.'

'Why influential as well as rich?' asked William.

27

'Because there could be vigorous objections from all the leading hotels when they realise what we are aiming to do!'

She started to talk about the island of Anguilla itself: low-lying, often windy, but quiet with wonderful beaches, it was ripe for more development. The year-round dry, sunny weather discouraged both cultivation of crops and raising of cattle. The main indigenous industry was catching fish and exporting them.

'So labour would not be a problem,' observed William.

Harold took the opportunity to excuse himself and make for the men's room.

'And what about you? What do *you* do?' Anne-Marie enquired.

William explained he was a London art dealer staying in Anguilla on holiday. Changing the subject, he said, 'I have only been in these parts once in my life before and you remind me very much of someone I met at the time. Did you ever have a sister living on Anguilla?'

'I did until recently,' Anne-Marie laughed. 'She was called Chloe. She, her husband and children now live in America. The husband's a pilot with an American airline. My daughter's a pilot too, incidentally. If you came in a private charter plane from Antigua, she could even have been *your* pilot!'

'Is she called Carmen? She certainly looked a bit like you.'

'That's her! Hope you weren't too terrified!' Then, after a pause: 'I've been trying to think where you might have met my sister. When you were in Anguilla last time, did you ever go to the house of some people called van Straaten? She used to work there.'

Before William could reply, Harold reappeared and interrupted them, informing Anne-Marie that he had just met some old friends from England sitting at one of the tables.

William's mind was going back twenty five years to his first visit, when he and his American host had spent two days and two nights with some friends of the American's at their villa on the other end of the island from where the American lived. Were they called van Straaten? William could not remember. 'Too far to drive there and back in the day...' his American friend had said.

Harold had subsequently monopolised the conversation and no more was said about the sister before they left to catch the ferry some ten minutes later. William could not constrain himself and once on board blurted out to his companion that he was sure he had met Anne-Marie's sister on his previous visit. 'On the two nights we were there, she was helping serve at dinner parties. Tall, good figure, with beautiful brown eyes. I noticed her right away. She noticed me too and we exchanged quite a number of glances!'

'Look, old boy,' Harold broke in. 'I'd love to hear the story, but with all this noise from the engine, couldn't we have another quiet evening on our own tonight? It would be more conducive. How do you know for certain it was the sister anyhow?'

So it was arranged that Harold would come to William's hotel at eight o'clock. William was much calmer and had planned to revert to the subject over coffee in the lounge later, but they had barely sat down at the table and given their orders before Harold told him to carry on with his story.

'I know it was the sister all right,' he began. 'She looked so much like Anne-Marie, same sort of face, same build.'

'Well, I used to know her and her family before they moved,' said Harold. 'You could almost have mistaken the two sisters for twins. Anyhow I believe they were only about a year apart in age. But there must be something more you want to tell me!'

'Well, yes ... if you swear to keep it to yourself.'

'I swear,' said Harold.

'On the second night, after the party had broken up and all of us staying had gone to bed, I was half asleep when I heard my door being opened. I didn't turn on the light ... I didn't do anything, but if it was an intruder I was ready to jump out at him. Then I heard a female voice call my name softly. Somehow I was sure it was her. I threw open the bed clothes and, as if in answer, I heard

30

the sound of clothes being removed and thrown on the floor.'

'And you hadn't discussed this venture between you in any way before?' interrupted Harold.

'No, I'd hardly spoken to her – just things like wishing her good evening when I'd run into her casually in the house. There were always other people around. But I'm sure she knew how I felt about her.'

'And then what happened?'

'It was the most marvellous experience I'd ever had in my life. We hardly exchanged a word. And she left far too soon, as quietly as she had come in.'

'Did you see her the following morning?'

'The man with whom I was staying on the island and I left early before any of the staff was around, not that I know if she even lived in. We'd said our goodbyes to our hosts the night before, so I couldn't even try and find out a bit about her from them.'

'Probably just as well you didn't,' remarked Harold thoughtfully. 'Never good to draw attention to yourself in circumstances such as you describe.'

The two men met again the next day. 'I got a shock when I saw that pilot, Carmen, at Antigua airport,' William said out of the blue. 'She looked so like the girl I was telling you about last night that I thought, I hope to hell that's not my daughter!'

'Come to think of it, she's got a bit of a look of you too!' said Harold.

'Thank you very much!' William exploded. 'She's Anne-Marie's daughter – I didn't seduce the two of them!'

'What did you think of Anne-Marie?' asked Harold. 'She told me once she married early, but it didn't work out. Husband never had a proper job, couldn't give her children etc., so they separated by mutual agreement. Evidently he's never been in touch since and she doesn't know where he is. But, this is the strange thing: after he'd left her and gone to live somewhere else, she found she was carrying a child.'

'Carmen?'

'Yes.'

After a while William said, 'You're an author. You've got imagination. What do you make of it?'

'Anne-Marie was probably very keen to have a child but knew no one she fancied marrying. Could she have taken the sister's position in that house while you were there?'

'Unlikely. The hosts would have noticed and even the guests seemed to know the sister well. And if Anne-Marie was on the look-out for a young, suitable prospect to father a child for her, how did she know who was coming?'

'Tricky ... I'll have to give it more thought,' concluded Harold. 'Anyway, Carmen could quite simply be the husband's daughter, conceived before he went away.'

They were both sitting in chairs on the beach of William's hotel. Eventually Harold rose to go, adding he would be in touch again soon.

William spent the next few days relaxing. He had had a long telephone conversation with Lady Canningstoke, who unfortunately seemed very enthusiastic about the property he had inspected on her behalf. He had been able to answer most of her questions, but that still left a list of three or four points to which he did not know the answer. So another visit to the old man living on the estate was called for. The first time he drove up there again, there was no answer to his ringing of the bell and no way he could gain access to go in and look for him. He tried again early the following day and was successful in that he met the man as he was coming out of the gates on his bicycle. He cheerfully answered William's questions more or less adequately. The one important point where he was unable to help was in giving an indication of the price the current owner was looking for.

'If you gave me your phone number, I could get the owner to ring you,' he said. 'There's one thing I ought to tell you though. There are some other people who are interested – they've been all over the place several times.'

'Are they people from around these parts?' William asked innocently.

'Yes, might try and turn it into a hotel – if they can get permission for all they want to do from the local authorities.'

So the asking price won't be exactly low, at this stage, William thought. He thanked the man for his assistance and slipped a few dollar notes into his hand.

Later that morning, when he calculated the time would be early evening in England, William rang up Lady Canningstoke. She was appreciative of the further information he had been able to obtain, but sounded surprised when he mentioned for the first time that another party was interested in the property. Did he know who they were? People interested in turning the place into a hotel, William said. Did she want him to speak to the owner and get a price indication? No, leave that for the moment, Lady Canningstoke replied. I need to talk to my contact over here. Let's leave it that I will ring you tomorrow.

William was sitting in the hotel bar that evening when Harold appeared. After ordering the visitor a drink, William told him how he had been doing further work on the possible purchase of the plantation. 'Any idea how high Anne-Marie and her friends would go to buy the property?' he asked.

'If they can get clearance on change of use and planning, I think they'll pay whatever it takes,' Harold answered. 'I've been over in St Martin again today and Anne-Marie opened up a bit more to me. She's certainly got some pretty high-powered individuals in with her.'

'Sounds as if my lady in England is not going to know where she stands for quite a little while,' said William. 'Did you get any more ideas on the other matter while you were over there?'

'It was really why I went, although it took me a long time to introduce the subject in a casual manner!'

'Well?'

'According to Anne-Marie, it wasn't the sister, Chloe, you had the moment of passion with, but her, Anne-Marie!

William was dumbstruck. 'So I could be the father of Carmen?' he said at last.

'According to her, you *are!*'

'Does Carmen know anything about this?'

'I don't think so.'

'How on earth was it fixed?'

'Can I have another drink and I'll tell you?' Harold said.

After the waiter had brought it, Harold took a long gulp and started his story: 'As I thought, Anne-Marie had always wanted a child. Chloe was aware of this and was keen to do anything she could to help her sister. For some time she had been keeping an eye out at the house where she worked – the one where you stayed for a couple of days – for a youngish man, preferably good-looking, who was visiting the island and hopefully unlikely to be coming back again, at any rate in the near future. Then she had to make herself reasonably sure that the young man was a bit of a sportsman, who would not be averse to some fun with a girl he fancied. She started flirting with you and could tell you were attracted...'

'I might have turned the light on,' interrupted William.

'They had to take that chance. Even then you might not have noticed ... if the girl turned her head away ... they were very alike. Anyway, she let her sister into the house during the evening.'

'My God!' said William. 'Had they done this sort of thing before?'

'According to Anne-Marie, no.'

'I'd better have another drink as well,' said William. 'I'm going to leave these parts as soon as I can. I certainly don't want to come face to face with Anne-Marie again!'

However, there was the problem of the Lady Canningstoke mission, he thought, lying awake in the night. He was fast asleep at eight o'clock in the morning when his telephone rang. It was Lady Canningstoke to say there was no more he could do and to thank him for all his help. She had been told she might have to wait some time before she could obtain an idea as to the price required.

William had become intrigued by Harold's story and was determined to have another look at Carmen. He motored to the airport and found the desk of the charter line on whose aircraft he had flown from Antigua. Yes, he could charter the plane for the following day. Yes, the pilot would be the same young lady who had flown him to Anguilla. He got them to reserve him a seat on the next connecting plane from Antigua to London. He then drove to Harold's house to say goodbye. Meeting him had certainly enlivened his stay and brought into the open the problems that would arise in trying to buy the plantation. Against that, admittedly in response to William's own curiosity, he had caused the visitor an alarming personal upset.

The next day, seated beside Carmen in the small plane, he studied her closely as she was preparing the plane for take-off. She had been her professional self when she collected him from the departure area, merely saying she hoped he had enjoyed his visit. Now he was looking at her to see if he could find any resemblance to himself. They did not speak much on the flight.

On arrival at Antigua, he thanked her for bringing him back as they shook hands.

She gave him a mischievous grin. 'It's been so nice meeting you after all these years,' she said.

At the Club

It was a bright, sunny morning and a perfect welcome to Hong Kong. I had arrived late the previous evening, and, taking my breakfast in the window of my room at the Mandarin Hotel, sitting high up in the sky, was enjoying watching the junks and sampans jostling with the cargo steamers in the channel between the island and the Chinese mainland. I should add that at the time, the Mandarin, the first of the new modern hotels to come, was the tallest building in the colony. Thirty years later, surrounded by more hotels and enormous office buildings, it would scarcely be remarked upon. Sadly, the wonderful view got lost too.

But this is beside the point. I was looking forward that day to my date with Charlie Watson, one of the English expatriate exporters for whom I acted in the United Kingdom. We were to meet for lunch at the Colonial Club, then still on its original site near the waterfront, overlooking the cricket ground. Charlie was a big, broad, ebullient character, who had become a close friend. On my arrival I was shown into the bar, and he came across to greet me with a wide grin on his ruddy face. We stood up at the bar where, without enquiring what I wanted, he ordered me a large pink gin. He introduced me to a couple of friends standing nearby, but eventually the two of us broke away and made our way to the dining-room. It felt good to be back in the noisy oak-panelled room and to receive the odd smiling glance of recognition.

As my host studied the wine list, I was struck by the handsome young European wine waiter by his side, standing out in the sea of Chinese waiters. Charlie wanted to order something special in my honour, and, after lengthy discussion, they agreed what to choose.

'He's French, name of Jean,' Charlie remarked when the man had gone. 'Son of one of the leading growers in the Bordeaux region. Over here for six months on some sort of exchange and seems very knowledgeable. In fact I've got him to come to my house Saturday night to be in charge of all the drinks at that party you're invited to. It's his evening off from the club.'

We had agreed that I should wait until the next day to visit Charlie in his office for the start of business discussions, so I decided to make use of a free afternoon by doing some shopping. The place I chose was Kowloon, on the other side of the straits, then – as now – a hubbub of Chinese traders, selling everything imaginable, although my particular plans were to seek out tailors and shirtmakers.

I remembered the Star Ferry Company provided a cross-harbour ferry service every eight minutes and I walked down to the terminus. The journey over the straits took ten minutes and I was soon amongst all the little shops. It must have been two hours later that I walked along to the Peninsula Hotel and sat down in the main lounge for a cup of tea. Looking round the room, I suddenly saw Jean, the wine waiter. He was sitting at a table with a girl, both of them talking and laughing. I was beside a tall fern in a Chinese pot, which I was pretty sure shielded me from any casual glances, so I was able to study the girl carefully: dark brown hair, with a beautiful, expressive face. Jean was in a smart blue suit and obviously enjoying himself. 'You're not wasting any time here, my lad,' I chuckled to myself. I left the lounge by a far door and walked back to the ferry.

The night of the party, I arrived early with my suitcase. Charlie had insisted I should stay the night. The house, which I had visited on previous trips, was a splendid affair, high up in the hills in the shadow of the Peak. The first guests were just arriving when I appeared downstairs in my dinner-jacket and I was soon in conversation with Charlie's wife, small, vivacious, dressed in an exquisite *cheongsam*. I saw Jean approaching with glasses of champagne on a tray.

'This is Jean,' the wife said to me, smiling, 'we've borrowed him for tonight from the club.'

'I already know the gentleman by sight,' Jean murmured, adding politely, 'I hope you have an enjoyable evening.'

As the early part of the evening progressed and the main reception room and adjoining terrace became crowded, I saw the Governor himself amongst the guests, mixing with Chinese couples and British people I knew by sight from the club. By chance I noticed Charlie's wife once or twice exchanging a look with the temporary employee. When the whole company eventually sat down for dinner at three long tables, Jean was even more to the fore, overseeing his many assistants pouring out the wine. I saw from the adjoining place-card that I had been put next to the Watsons' daughter, whom I remembered from some years before as a rather hefty, awkward teenager.

As she sat down a few minutes later and introduced herself, I recognised the girl I had seen at the Peninsula Hotel.

'It's such fun having him here,' she remarked, noticing Jean behind the far side of the table. 'I've met him a couple of times before – at a disco in the town where I sometimes go.'

The dinner and the accompanying wines were both excellent. The daughter, whose name was Sarah, had spent the last two years completing her education in London and Paris and barely stopped talking. In fact, I fear I rather neglected the lady on my other side. Coffee was being served when dancing commenced in another room and Sarah got up. She did not return and I was left talking to the other guests still at the table.

The party began to break up around midnight. I was having a dance with Charlie's wife when I saw Sarah again, dancing with a young man and full of high spirits. She gave me a little wave.

I congratulated Charlie on the success of the party and sat with him for a little while over a brandy. I then excused myself and went up to my room.

I awoke about three o'clock with a parched throat. The water in the basin in my room was tepid and I decided to go downstairs to see if I could find something a bit colder. Feeling my way through the main reception room, I noticed a man's shape asleep on one of the settees. I knew a small bar lay beyond, and once inside, turned on the light. I found a cold jug of water in a fridge. I was pouring it out into a glass when Jean appeared in the doorway.

'Oh, it's you,' he said. 'I heard a noise and came to see what it was.'

As I returned upstairs through the darkened sitting-room, I heard a distinct movement from behind the settee, where someone else – apparently – had been lying.

* * *

43

Working in my room a few mornings later, I was surprised when the hall porter rang to tell me there was a lady downstairs enquiring for me. On going into the hall I recognised Eva, Charlie Watson's wife, sitting in a chair. She rose and explained she'd been doing some shopping and thought she'd call in on me for a coffee. We went into the lounge and sat down.

After some rather strained small talk, Mrs Watson came to the point of her visit. 'It was me you may have heard in our sitting-room the other night when you came down for water,' she said. 'I was there ... to be with Jean.'

I made no reply and waited for her to continue. I had given little thought to the noise I had heard, but if I had, I would have supposed the other presence to have been that of Sarah.

'I know it's madness at my age, but I'm hopelessly in love with him,' she went on, 'and I just don't know what to do next. I've really come here to see if *you* have got any advice for me. I certainly don't want to discuss it with anyone I know locally. It would be all round Hong Kong in five minutes.'

'Do you feel he's in love with you?' I asked.

'Well, he says he is. But I don't know ... I sometimes wonder what could come of it anyhow, with the age difference.'

'Eva,' I said at length, 'the only advice I can give you is to drop him and not see him again. Think how you would hurt Charlie if he found out and, just as bad, if it became public knowledge. Doubtless it will be painful, but it is your only course of action.'

'I rather expected you to say that, I suppose,' she replied, stifling some tears. 'But I've been so desperate, I just had to confide in someone.'

In a little while I escorted her to the door of the hotel. Her eyes, her whole demeanour, showed that she was distraught and she had a strange look on her face as we parted. I only hope you don't find out he's been carrying on with your daughter as well, I thought to myself.

I received a further shock a few days later when, lunching at the club again with Charlie, he told me that Sarah had told him she and Jean wanted to marry. Jean himself was nowhere to be seen that day, but Charlie told me he was on sick leave.

'What does Eva feel about it?' I asked as casually as possible.

'Like me, obviously got reservations,' Charlie said. 'In fact, I think she's very much against it. Keeps telling me she can't believe it.'

We talked a little more on the subject, but then moved on to other matters. I did not see Charlie again before I left Hong Kong the following week, but spoke to him on the telephone to say goodbye. He told me in passing there was a big to-do going on at the club. One of their most valuable possessions, an engraved gold cup donated to mark the accession of King George V by Sir Roy Wang Chi Po, the first mega-rich Chinese taipan, had gone missing.

'He couldn't become a member of course on account of his nationality,' he said, 'but I suppose it was his way of telling the committee he was as good as any of them – probably better,' he laughed. 'Anyway, they could hardly refuse it, and it has been kept in a locked glass case in the committee room ever since. Strange thing is, the case was still locked but empty – a cleaning woman first noticed its disappearance.'

'Wouldn't it be very difficult to dispose of?' I ventured.

'A thief could find a rich buyer all right in Canton,' Charlie replied, 'although there would be the trouble of getting it there through two lots of customs. More likely, the plan would be to get it melted down here. Its not all that big, but solid eighteen carat.'

'By the way, is Jean back?'

'Hasn't returned to the club. And he hasn't kept in touch with Sarah which he promised to. She thought he might have met with an accident, but the British hospital knew nothing about him.'

'Do you think there might be a connection?'

'Between what?'

'The theft and Jean's absence.'

Charlie seemed surprised at my question. 'He comes from a rich background. Why should he need the money? Unless he's been gambling and is under pressure from Chinese bookmakers. They can be pretty abrasive if they want to be, I believe.'

His last remarks were made in a jocular, dismissive manner, with which he obviously intended to close the conversation; so we made our farewells and I rang off.

I wouldn't have known any more about these parochial troubles, or at least not until the distant future when I was again in Hong Kong, had not Charlie unexpectedly called in on me at my London office a few months later. He was on his way to see his distributor in New York and spending a couple of days in London on the way.

We discussed some business matters and then he suddenly said, 'They found the gold cup, by the way. The police got a warrant to search Jean's room and they found it hidden there.'

'But what on earth made them suspect him?'

'He was one of the few who would have had access to the glass case. The key hung along with the key to the wine cellar and some other keys to various cabinets on a small enclosed board in the secretary's office. The police wanted to know the names of everybody who would have been able to open up the board. In fact there was next to nobody, but they even insisted on seeing me, as the secretary was obliged to tell them that as chairman of the wine committee I had a key to the board on my key-ring, so I could get hold of the key to the wine cellar. It's one of the chairman's duties to make regular checks on the stock,' he added by way of explanation.

'I hope they didn't think someone in your house borrowed your key-ring when you weren't wearing it and obtained access to the key-board!' I remarked facetiously.

'If you're implying my daughter had something to do with it,' replied Charlie angrily, 'she broke off with Jean and wrote to him at his rooming house saying she wanted to end their engagement. She hadn't heard a word and nobody knew where he was. She'd established he'd kept his room on though.'

I apologised profusely for my stupid remark and said I was only joking.

'Jean turned up again at the club eventually,' continued Charlie. 'Had some marvellous excuse that he'd had a fall while he was in a weak state and been badly concussed – even claimed to have sent a message through. Anyway, he could prove he'd been in some Chinese hospital. I spent a good hour with him one morning, checking the wine inventory with all the bottles in the cellar and he seemed quite normal, and very shocked about the theft. You see, I just wanted to make sure the thief hadn't helped himself to a few bottles of wine as well.'

'How often did Jean need to go down to the wine cellar? It would be time consuming having to ask the secretary or whoever to open up the board each time. Surely the wines for everyday drinking are all kept upstairs, either being kept cool somewhere or – in the case of the reds – in those big racks in the dining-room.'

'Traditionally the wine waiter has always had access to the cellar key whenever he wanted, partly to stock up and also in case a member wants a bottle of one of our old vintage clarets, which he'd have to go down and get.'

'So where's Jean now?' I asked.

'Well, earlier on, the police had questioned him, even held him overnight, but got nowhere. He told them to search his room and they found nothing. Then they had an anonymous tip-off and had another go. So now he's in custody and still proclaiming his innocence. He got back from work one afternoon after the lunchtime session and found the police waiting for him. He made out he was absolutely amazed when they told him where they had found it – behind a pile of shirts and sweaters at the top of a cupboard. Why hadn't they found it the first time? He'd got it hidden somewhere else, they said. But, I ask you, who else could have stolen it and what would be the point of putting it in Jean's room? The court's in recess at the moment, but when his case comes up, I could see him getting a nasty jail sentence. Don't envy him spending time in a Hong Kong jail,' Charlie added grimly.

I sat silently while Charlie, after a pause, went on: 'Funnily enough, my wife had been at the

49

club the day before it was noticed the cup was missing. She goes there every two weeks out of the goodness of her heart, early in the morning before it opens officially, to clean the gold and silver items – they're mainly in the locked cases – and I'd lent her my key to the board in the usual way. They don't trust the Chinese to do it after one of them dropped something. She's completely devastated about the whole thing, poor dear.'

It was only after Charlie had left that I started to wonder at the possible significance of some lines of William Congreve.

Heaven has no rage like love to hatred turn'd,
Nor Hell a fury like a woman scorn'd.

On Safari

The notice inside sternly admonished passengers not to leave the minibus in the event of emergency and here they were, standing in the bush with night falling, as the driver struggled to free a trapped rear wheel. Some of the male passengers were pushing from behind. They were on their way from the local airstrip to a lodge in the Masai Mara.

Composed of writers, journalists and public figures, the party had been put together by the Ministry of Tourism to help promote the newly emerging safari holidays. Harry Eastwood was a struggling, virtually unknown novelist and had not been his publishers' first choice when they had been approached in London, but with two of their leading authors uninterested, they had put his name forward. The recommendation had been accepted without query by the Ministry. Harry himself was keen enough on the prospect of a free holiday and accordingly found himself in the business class of a plane to Nairobi a few weeks later. Tall, trim, fair hair, in his early thirties and unmarried, he was about to have the sort of far-flung holiday he could never have afforded himself.

There were seven other members of the party and Harry made a point of introducing himself to each one when they were gathered together in the VIP lounge at Heathrow airport. Sadly for him, his fellow travellers were all – at least by their own lights and in their own fields – reasonably well-known. One thing they all knew was that they had never heard of Harry. So, although perfectly polite, no one went out of his or her way to become overtly friendly.

The mishap on the bus solved, the party eventually arrived at the lodge. They found the accommodation consisted of a sprawling collection of huts and tents around the main building, a one-storey affair housing a large lounge cum dining-room. The whole area was enclosed by a high wire fence. Cocktails and beer were offered before dinner, and bottles of wine were on the table when they came to sit down at the long table around two pots of lamb stew. With all the food and drink and the friendliness of the staff – Africans dressed in khaki tunics with red cummerbunds and long khaki trousers – a relaxed atmosphere pervaded when the young English girl, who had received them on arrival, came and sat down. She was in charge of the safaris, she explained, in the temporary absence of her superior. Well-built, broad-shouldered, with a few locks of short blonde hair tumbling down on her forehead, she started to tell them about plans for the following day and to explain correct conduct out in the bush. There seemed to be no other people in the lodge. Tired, Harry slipped away after the talk had finished and made his way to the small hut he had been allocated.

He had already unpacked his things and without undressing lay down on his bed. He gazed idly at a notice on the wall warning visitors not to venture into the compound if they heard a siren blowing. This was to indicate an animal had somehow gained access. What kind of animal, he wondered? A cat shot out from under his bed. He shooed it out the door, and checking under the bed to make sure there was nothing else lurking there, pulled out from off the floor a small cracked black and white photograph. It was of a small boy with his hand on the head of a young lion. Left there by a previous occupant, he imagined, and he tucked it into the side of a mirror standing on a dresser. He had a night of fitful sleep, hearing distant noises of wild animals calling and grunting.

Back in the main room at the lodge for breakfast, the other travellers – despite the general joviality of the night before – had become taciturn again, even amongst themselves. Harry was relieved when, on reporting beside the two four-wheel drive vehicles parked outside, he was told to get into the first one, which was evidently to contain the woman in charge. At least he would have the presence of an attractive girl. Three other passengers were allocated to this vehicle, two middle-aged journalists from rival broadsheet London papers, who seemed to know each other, and a stout lady of certain years whom he had heard of as a detective story writer. The interior of the vehicle had been adapted so that two people sat each side, one behind the other. The girl, Christine, introducing herself for the first time, sat at the wheel. Beside her sat a tough-looking Masai Moran, in khaki with green fez, holding a rifle.

The main gates of the compound were opened and it was not long before they encountered a herd of impala. Giraffes peered at them from afar over dried-up trees. Ten minutes later, and close by, were herds of gazelle and zebra. Baboons stared at them, standing in the car's path. It was when they veered off the track and started to motor over scrubland that Christine told them to keep silent and as still as possible. She was looking for a particular lion, she said, which she knew inhabited that area. After an hour driving round in bigger and bigger circles, instead they came upon a cheetah. It was busy eating a recently caught impala, and the passengers had time to snap away with their cameras before it ran on.

They never found the lion that morning, but having dropped the African off at a native compound, Christine invited Harry to come and sit beside her up front for the rest of the drive back to the lodge. They were soon into a cheery conversation.

'I'm rather the odd one out here,' remarked Harry. 'I don't know any of the others.'

'I noticed you were rather keeping yourself to yourself,' Christine said. 'I thought you were just shy.'

'Not really,' laughed Harry. 'I must start making a bit more of an effort. '

He managed to get himself beside the girl again that afternoon, when the party was being taken to look at the hippos in the river near where the camp was based. Diving under the water, snaking around, they flashed their big eyes menacingly. That evening a short safari was organised – this time Harry was in the other vehicle – and then the tourists were asked to assemble in the lounge to be told about an expedition by balloon early the following morning. What with the six o'clock start and doubts about going up in a balloon, only four people let their names go forward: Harry, one of the two journalists, a middle-aged woman whom Harry knew to be an actress and an older man who turned out to be a Member of Parliament.

When the time came, the small party plus Christine and a member of the African staff made its way to an area just outside the compound where a large red and blue balloon had previously landed. The six of them climbed into the basket, greeted by the young native in charge, and with a hissing escape of gas, the balloon rose steadily into the air. Another balloon was to come later with the supplies for a champagne breakfast. The sun was starting to rise as they soared up into the heavens. Looking down, Harry saw the clusters of animals and the limitless view of wild, flat country.

The balloon drifted steadily along and eventually came to rest a dozen miles away near a river. The visitors climbed out awkwardly, half falling over as their feet touched the ground. A rifle Harry had noticed earlier was left in the basket, so he assumed the tour was more for appreciation of the scenic panorama than to get near dangerous beasts. Christine's assistant started to pour out mugs of tea.

They noticed another balloon, which had landed a little way off on the other side of the river.

'That's our breakfast,' Christine remarked, waving and shouting at the occupants. The balloon started to ascend. Crossing the river at low altitude, the basket brushed the trees on either side, and then landed a hundred yards away. Two Africans pulled out wicker baskets, laughing and shouting as they brought them across.

The breakfast was laid out on a large tablecloth on the ground and the journalist wasted little time in complying with Christine's suggestion to open the champagne.

'How's your fellow newspaperman going to be able to write up this little jaunt?' Harry asked, as his glass was being filled. 'The sheer desolation is really beautiful at this time of day.'

'How's he going to write it up?' the journalist laughed. 'Don't worry – knowing him, he's already done it, complete with "eerie morning light" or some such nice touch.'

The actress and the Member of Parliament were improving fast on a casual relationship struck up at the lodge, with the MP laughing delightedly at the actress's remarks. Half an hour later, the two of them wandered off for a stroll along the river. 'Don't go too far!' Christine called out after them. She motioned to the native assistant to follow at a discreet distance.

The journalist had partaken amply of the offerings of sausage, ham, cheese, rolls and jam, not to mention the champagne, and was having a quiet doze with his back leaning on the balloon's basket. Christine and Harry were still seated on the ground around the tablecloth.

All morning Harry had been observing her and become more and more attracted. With hair tucked under a peaked cap, in a light khaki safari suit, her businesslike competence only added to her physical charm. Out of the blue, he said softly, 'I wish we could see each other again – after this trip, I mean. That is presuming you haven't got a steady boyfriend somewhere.' Christine gave no reaction and he began to regret his daring.

Eventually she turned towards him, meeting his eyes in a friendly way. Was it possible she could be harbouring a feeling similar to his own? He was not bad-looking, he thought, going through his good points.

'Yes, I'd like that,' she said.

The journalist had roused himself and was wandering over towards them. Harry continued to gaze at the girl, but knew he must change the conversation. 'Something I've been meaning to ask you,' he said, suddenly finding a subject, 'do you recall who was in my room at the lodge before me? I found an old photograph of a child with a lion and wondered who it belonged to.'

Was it his imagination or did Christine look away from him and towards the approaching journalist a little too quickly?

She was on her feet with a smile at the journalist. 'I must see about getting us all back,' she announced. 'It's not too pleasant being up in a balloon in the heat of the day. Now, where are the others?'

The couple concerned were on their way back, with the assistant in tow. She signalled to them to hurry. The two Africans from the other balloon came to gather up the remains of the breakfast.

She walked over to the main balloon and told the driver to prepare for departure.

'I can tell you about that photo,' she had said in a whisper, standing beside him in the basket of the balloon on the way back. 'Be in your room at ten o'clock tonight.'

Safely back, all the balloon passengers had decided that they had had enough activity for one day and were going to sit out on the veranda or rest on their beds until dinner time. Now it was ten o'clock in the evening and Harry was sitting in his small hut waiting for the girl to come.

A few minutes later, there was a quiet knock, and simultaneously, the door opened a fraction and Christine slipped through.

'Had to be careful I wasn't seen,' she smiled. 'And we must talk quietly!'

Harry took hold of her, but she pushed him away gently, saying, 'Show me this photo. Where did you find it?

'Well, it didn't belong to a guest,' Christine said, sitting down on the one chair and frowning at the photo, gesturing to him to sit down on the bed. 'This picture is of a man called Bill, who until recently was in charge of the safaris, in fact of the whole camp. I worked with him and for the moment at any rate I've taken over his job. This room is where he lived.

'He was brought up at this place. It was only a small house and compound in those days, of course, but it was the way his father liked to live.

59

His father gave him school lessons in the morning, and in the afternoons they used to go out looking at all the wild life, looking after them as well if anything needed an injury attending to. I gather most of the animals got to know them pretty well – at least the animals weren't frightened of them. Bill would have been about ten when this photograph was taken.'

'But how did the two of them survive?' Harry asked curiously.

'Bill told me they drove into the nearest town once a week for provisions. In an emergency, the father had his radio telephone.'

A strange life for a young child, Harry thought.

'Bill was about nineteen when his father died,' Christine went on. 'It was he who got the government backing to turn the place into a tourist lodge.'

'And where is he now, this "temporarily absent" superior you mentioned on our first night?'

'That's the mystery. Three weeks ago he disappeared. Just vanished without saying anything to anybody and we haven't heard a word since. He had his own vehicle here, an old Land Rover, which we never used for trekking, and he must have made off in that. After a few days, I rang up the man we come under in Nairobi and I know he organised a search of the area, but nothing was found.'

'Do you think he wanted to start a new life somewhere else?'

'A strange way of going about it. What hit me more than anything was that we had both become … close and … well, he never gave me any hint as to what he might be up to. Except…'

A surge of jealousy had gone through Harry at the mention of their becoming close. It was only after a pause that he said, 'Except what?'

Harry noticed Christine was beginning to look ill at ease. Shuffling around in her chair, she said, 'Once or twice he'd said to me it was a pity things weren't like they used to be … when he lived here with his father, I suppose. I didn't take him very seriously. Then one night a lion managed to break into a stockade belonging to a tribe near here. It was full of cows and goats shut up for the night; they only let them wander around during the day. The natives knew the lion; he had tried to get in once or twice before, but unsuccessfully. Actually it was amazing he *did* get in, the way the locals arrange the barricades. But he'd forced the main gate open. The cows and goats panicked and stampeded out. He'd killed and started eating several of them before the natives managed to drive him away. Anyhow, a lot of pressure was put on us to do something. Bill got on to Nairobi and was told to cull the culprit without delay.'

'And did he?'

'He lay up there for three nights, and on the third night he got him. The next few days he was

61

very morose and hardly spoke. The staff here put it down to shock.'

'And I suppose he packed his things and pushed off soon after,' Harry said. 'It must have been a bit traumatic to have had to do that after the sort of upbringing he'd had. Although you would have thought he'd have realised he might be called on to do something of that nature one day.'

'Killing the lion could have been the reason,' Christine said thoughtfully. 'It's been worrying me though and I'd got no one to talk to about it.'

'Well, you've got it off your chest now with me,' Harry said briskly. 'Try and put it out of your mind.' He was eager to bring the conversation back to the few words they had exchanged sitting by the balloon. 'Look, did you mean it about our seeing each other again?'

Christine began to speak in a very unemotional, matter-of-fact tone. 'After your party goes the day after tomorrow, we've got no more guests for a week and I'm going to take some leave and have a few days in Nairobi. In fact, I'm coming back as far as Nairobi with all of you. What about staying on a bit yourself and taking a later plane back to London? I saw on your details you're an author so presumably you don't have to rush back to some job!'

She was getting to her feet as Harry crossed the small space towards her. He grasped her and their lips met. 'I must go now,' she said after a short while. He kissed her again before she went quietly out of the door.

Harry could hardly sleep thinking about his amazing good fortune. On the two safaris the next day, although they were both in the same vehicle, they barely spoke. They found a beautiful lioness sitting by a tree with her cubs, but again no sight of a lion. That night she joined them all for dinner and once their eyes met briefly.

By minibus from the reserve to the air strip and then into the small plane, the party – including Christine – arrived at Nairobi airport late the following morning. Harry had already announced to the other guests that he would not be returning home with them, but planned to spend a few days in the capital to absorb some local colour for a forthcoming book. Nobody was particularly interested. When he was busy at an airline counter trying to change his ticket to London, Christine walked over to say goodbye, shaking hands ostentatiously. She told him to meet her at a certain hotel in central Nairobi.

Harry took a taxi into town, and going into the lounge of the hotel, saw Christine sitting over a coffee.

'Darling,' he said, taking her hand.

Ever businesslike, Christine said, 'I've got myself a large double room here. Are you happy sharing with me?'

'I'll go and register and get my luggage sent up. What number is it?'

They both started to laugh.

'I think I saw Bill this afternoon,' Christine said as they were settling down for dinner that evening in a restaurant that had recently won a local award. She had insisted on an afternoon's shopping on her own, while Harry had wandered around the streets in the old quarter, looking at all the merchandise spread out for sale on the pavements.

'He was in a shop where I was buying some new boots. At least, I'm pretty sure it was him. But when I looked again he had vanished. I don't know whether he saw me. I wonder if he knows he's officially listed as a missing person.'

Harry gave her a worried look. 'Should you report that you've seen him?' he asked.

'No. I don't know for certain it was him and anyhow what help would it be?'

They started to talk of other things and were both in a carefree mood when they regained the hotel and their bedroom. For the first time that day Harry started making serious love to Christine, kissing her face and feeling her body. They were standing together undressing when they fell on the bed. Christine was a passionate girl and not without experience. Harry gave full rein to his own feelings.

* * *

Much, much later – they had got up and washed, tidied their clothes off the floor, the light was off – Harry was woken by a definite movement in the room. He had no idea of the time, but he could see it was still dark outside. First, he wondered how anybody could have got in. Then he realised he had no recollection of locking the door and he doubted if Christine would have done so. He whispered Christine's name but she was sleeping peacefully. He fumbled for the bedside light, and as it came on, he saw a man going out of the door. Naked, jumping from the bed, Harry ran after him out into the corridor. He caught up with him by the lifts and grabbed his shirt.

'What the hell do you think you're doing?' he shouted. 'And who are you?'

The man was about his own age and dressed in a shirt and shorts. He tried to wriggle free, but a taller and determined Harry had now got him in an arm lock and was holding him fiercely.

A loud shriek came from behind them. 'Bill!' It was Christine's voice. She had woken, found the bedroom door open, thrown on a dressing-gown and rushed out into the passage.

'Did you break into our room? What do you want?'

'If you will tell your friend to release my arm, we might all talk,' the man replied.

'All right,' said Harry, 'but try to run off and I'll *really* let you have it.'

'I just wanted to speak to you,' the man said, addressing Christine. 'I didn't know you would have somebody with you.'

'Well, it's an odd time of the day, or rather night, to try and see me,' Christine replied calmly. 'I'm certainly not getting into any conversation with you now. But if you would like to be in the coffee shop downstairs between nine and ten in the morning, I may be in a better mood.'

Harry had his finger on the lift button, and when the lift came, he pushed the man into it. As they walked back to their room, an elderly couple in night attire were standing in a doorway, eyeing the girl and the naked man. Harry and Christine didn't offer any explanation.

They locked and bolted their door. 'He must have been half drunk breaking in on us like that,' remarked Christine drowsily, as they lay in each other's arms. 'Anyway, we'll see what he wants in the morning – that's if he turns up.' Sleep eventually enveloped them both.

Christine was the first to wake in the morning. 'It's nine o'clock,' she cried. 'We must go down and see if he's there.' They dressed hurriedly, and on reaching the coffee shop, saw Bill sitting at a table. With no apology or explanation for his earlier behaviour, Bill came to the point without ado.

'I want to know whether you'll support me on something I am planning to do,' he said, looking at Christine. 'I think you knew I was not too happy about life at our lodge the way it is now, and that business with the lion made up my mind. I want to destroy the whole compound ... put things back as they used to be.'

He did not go on, and trying to humour him, a puzzled Christine asked, 'What good would that do? There are plenty of other lodges throughout Kenya, and in Masai Mara itself for that matter.'

'I want to see the animals really free again, with no one chasing them around in vehicles. Go back to being wild like they are supposed to be,' said Bill, back again in full flow. 'And it would only need one lodge to be set ablaze for tourist business to die down in all the others. I could see the whole lot being closed down.'

Christine and Harry exchanged a look. Freshly shaved, hair brushed down, neat in a well-pressed lightweight suit, Bill appeared the very opposite of the scruffy individual they had encountered a few hours earlier. But Harry was thinking that, after several weeks of ruminating alone and wallowing in self-doubt, Bill's mind was perhaps running off course ... becoming unbalanced.

'And why are you telling *me* all this?' asked Christine.

Bill gave Christine a quiet look, without answering. Harry started to wonder, dispassionately this time, not jealously, how close they had been. Had

67

they been lovers? Had Christine once shared Bill's wild ideas?

'I want nothing to do with it,' Christine went on. 'I should be reporting you to the Ministry. Do you know they've got you down as a missing person? You should report to them and resign your position. And don't let me see you anywhere near *our* camp. Where are you living now, anyhow?'

'I'm sorry, I thought I'd found in you a fellow free-thinker, that we could achieve something worthwhile together,' Bill said evenly, rising from the table.

An unsettled Harry had immediately begun questioning Christine. Face tense, she had admitted, yes, they had been more than close; even marriage had been discussed. She had sympathised with his feelings, but never, never agreed to be a party to any mad schemes – not that he had ever put anything specific into words. She professed herself horrified at what he was now talking about; wanted nothing more to do with him.

'One thing's for sure,' Harry had ended by saying. 'I'm not going to let you go back to the camp on your own.'

Christine went to see her man at the Ministry of Tourism later the same morning. 'How can we trace him in Nairobi?' the official asked. 'Do you know where he's staying?' It was agreed the Ministry would put the police station in the camp's nearest town on alert, and that she, the one currently in charge of the camp, should return forthwith. The official would co-opt an experienced man to join her as soon as possible. He gave her a special telephone number to ring if she needed the police and told her she must explain the situation to the staff, particularly the guards and night-watchmen, with instructions to be extra vigilant. Christine was gratified that, whilst offering little practical help immediately, the man was at least taking her seriously.

Harry resolved to hire a self-drive car to take them back to the reserve, and directly the Ministry's appointee arrived, he intended to return to Nairobi and fly home. He had a book to finish in England, and in any event, in the midst of her sea of troubles, he found his ardour towards Christine, unfairly perhaps, cooling.

Very early the next morning they were on the road. In the camp everything was quiet, with no guests expected for several more days. Christine established contact by radio telephone with the local police chief and called all the African staff together. They were startled to hear the chain of events and vowed to be on the look-out for possible trouble.

That evening, as Harry was reading quietly in the lounge of the main building, an alarmed Christine rushed in to tell him she had spotted

Bill's Land Rover half hidden in some trees on the other side of the wire surround.

'I'm going out to see if he's sitting there,' she exclaimed. 'I've got to see what he's up to.'

'I'll come with you,' Harry said, getting to his feet.

'No, it's better if I handle him on my own. I'll try and get him to come inside.'

An anxious Harry waited, pacing the room. Half an hour later, he was about to go out to see what was happening, when Christine reappeared, with Bill following.

Bill was the first to speak. 'Christine's agreed to marry me,' he announced to a startled Harry. 'In the time since you last saw me I have realised I love her above all else. I am giving up all thought of changing things here in Kenya.'

'How can you be sure he means what he says?' Harry addressed Christine. 'About giving up his plans, I mean.'

One of the servants appeared in the room, looking at Bill with amazement. 'It's all right,' Christine reassured him. 'Just get us all some drinks.'

Telling Bill to sit at the long table, she drew Harry aside.

'I must stand by him,' she said softly. 'He's going to try and get official approval for re-instatement. He might get it and he might not, but I want to be with him. He's the only man I've ever truly been in love with.'

She added this last remark with tears in her eyes. She moved away to the table. Left alone with his thoughts, Harry's first reaction was to marvel at her complete disregard for what his own feelings might have become. Then he determined that, at any rate, he would refuse to let Bill have his old room back that night, because he, Harry, was occupying it. Only after that did he ponder over how ridiculous the situation had become. Christine seemed to have taken very little time to become convinced of Bill's good intentions. Were they an elaborate bluff and, if so, how would everything end up?

The servant had laid out drinks on the table, and as Harry joined the two of them, he had to admit that Bill seemed to be behaving quite naturally. Conversation was stilted, however, and after a light meal was served, Harry pleaded fatigue and retired to his hut. He vowed to leave early the next morning. 'Hope I'm not going to be burnt alive in my bed,' was his final thought as he dropped off to sleep.

Back in England, Harry was dozing over a Sunday newspaper a few weeks later, when a headline caught his eye: 'Mystery Fire at Kenyan Safari Lodge'. As he read on, it became clear that the lodge in question was the lodge where he had stayed. Many buildings were damaged; it had been temporarily closed down. The Kenyan police were investigating: 'arson had not been ruled out.' They were interviewing all the staff, including several who had been seriously burned. They were eager to talk to a white male supervisor, who was missing from the compound.

There were no more details. No word about a white female. Harry hoped she wasn't one of those who had been seriously burned. Maybe she was an unharmed survivor. Or was she – he hardly dared contemplate it – like her lover, also 'missing from the compound'?

Robby

Not all corners of the famous film actor Sir Robert Sheldon's early days are touched upon in his recent autobiography. To digress for a moment, when the subject of an autobiography came up, 'Robby' Sheldon had to admit that his schooldays had perhaps been over occupied with dreaming about the future and how he might put to advantage his good looks. Leaving school at sixteen, he realised that learning to write, even learning to spell, were subjects it might have paid him to concentrate on more diligently. When it came to writing a book, he would need plenty of help from somebody else.

The approach had come from a firm of London publishers, after he had given up his stint of seven impersonations of Dumas' hero, d'Artagnan, in the famous series of films about 'The Three Musketeers'. Flattered, he had agreed readily enough, but had to make clear he would not find it easy putting his experiences to paper. Unfazed, the suave publisher told him there would be no difficulty about that. He would just have to provide his recollections – preferably containing some interesting, hopefully even contentious items about other well-known people in his profession. The publisher would put at his disposal, for as long as it took, a man who would write his story down for him, or, as it turned out, what portions of it Robby decided to relate.

Thus some details of his life were omitted: like, for instance, when he received his call-up papers for the army in 1944, aged eighteen. He had been fortunate enough to find work in the theatre since leaving school and the last thing he wanted was to join the army. Or at any rate not until he was ready and it suited him. He had been thinking about a plan of postponement and when one day he found the expected letter instructing him to report to a medical board, he went into action. In the house in Chiswick where he lived in one room with kitchen and use of bathroom, he had got to know a young man of almost exactly the same age by the name of Sexton, an overweight misfit who worked in a local shop. The landlady was in the habit of leaving the morning's post for all her tenants on a table just inside the front door. Robby started to make a point of being first down each morning to check the mail. Sexton's call-up notice had certainly not arrived on the same day as his own, but within a few days he duly found a similar buff envelope addressed to Mr Sexton, with '*The War Office*' printed on the back and an address to use for non-delivery. He took the letter up to his room and opened the envelope carefully. The letter was telling Sexton to report for medical examination on the same day and at the same place as he himself had been instructed. He resealed the envelope, went downstairs and put it back on the hall table.

Robby knew at what time Sexton usually returned from work, and the following day he hung around in the hall waiting to see him. He cheerily informed him he had been called up.

'Same as me,' replied Sexton, 'though they'll probably refuse me with my asthma.'

Robby had observed this condition on previous occasions. It was also very apparent that Sexton was mentally a little retarded.

On the due date, they arranged to go to the medical board together. They took the tube to Earls Court and walked to Cromwell Road. On arrival, they were shown into a room where they joined a queue in front of two clerks in army uniform, who took down their details from the letters they had brought with them. They were each handed a form to have ready for the medical examination. After being moved on to a changing room, they were instructed to strip down to their underpants and proceed to the medical room. They then stood in another queue together, one behind the other, to await so-called examination by various doctors, who sat behind tables and occasionally stirred themselves to listen to hearts and lungs through a stethoscope. The culmination was an appearance in front of an elderly, monocled gentleman in a blue pin-striped suit, standing on his own, who, after looking at teeth, eyes and in the ears, was telling each conscript to take down his pants, turn round and bend over.

'Bend over more,' he grunted at Robby, to the latter's embarrassment.

Robby had not enjoyed the experience of parading semi-naked with dozens of other young men and was glad to get his clothes on again. Sexton appeared similarly relieved, because he had not relished the cold in the unheated room. It had brought on his asthma, a condition which one of the doctors had noticed.

As Robby had anticipated, Sexton was pronounced unfit. He had not been labelled 'C3', the popular aphorism of the time, but, more mysteriously, 'B4'. He could expect a possible call for Auxiliary Fire Service duties, but the army had no use for him. Robby was accepted into the army without any reservations and would be told where to report in due course. When they were each sent their letters the following week, Robby had taken

Sexton's one. It was not too difficult to alter them. With a typewriter rubber and a bit of work on his old portable – similar print to the ancient machine the army was using – Robby's letter became Sexton's. Sexton was called up and told to stand by. The envelope addressed to Sexton went back on the hall table, and, for good measure, Robby altered Sexton's letter of rejection so that it was addressed to him.

Robby was acting as assistant stage manager and playing a small part in a play that had opened at the Arts Theatre. It was by a new, very young dramatist and had received ecstatic reviews in two of the highbrow Sunday papers. Despite this, business had been slow and was only just starting to pick up. After the show, before going back to his room in Chiswick, Robby had taken to going for a drink in a pub near the theatre.

He started talking to a girl he had seen there before, but never spoken to. She was short and dark, with close-cropped hair.

'Why aren't you in uniform?' she asked in a not unfriendly fashion.

'I've got one at home. Do you want me to go and get it?'

Two military policemen – red-caps, as they were known – were standing up at the bar. One of them approached him. He felt in his pocket for the letter he always carried, the one originally addressed to Sexton, stating his unsuitability for service. But the man only wanted to say that he had seen his play at a recent matinee and how much he had enjoyed it.

'So you're an actor,' the girl said. 'What are you in?'

She had seen the play but evidently did not remember *him*.

Robby and the girl, whose name was Fay, were talking and laughing, standing each other drinks, and Robby only noticed how the time was passing when the landlord started to chant 'time gentlemen please.'

'I'd better be getting back home,' he said.

'Where do you live?'

'Chiswick.'

She was the same age as he, eighteen, and working as an usherette in a Leicester Square cinema on a shift from midday until early evening. She was planning to join the WRNS.

'You can come and stay the night with me, if you like,' she said. 'I've got a room in a flat the other side of Cambridge Circus. It's not far to walk.'

Seeing Robby's look of surprise, she added: 'No monkey business, mind. *You* sleep on the divan.'

Dead tired, he was soon fast asleep. In the morning Fay was already up when he awoke. He thanked her for putting him up and they agreed to meet again. She did not ask him any more about his not being in one of the services. In point of fact, when the play ended, he planned to join up. He would go to a recruiting station, give his correct name and show his identity card. Meanwhile, in case there was any trouble brewing over that letter he had altered, he had moved accomodation to another address in Chiswick.

Billy Sexton had been in a more muddled state of mind than usual since his arrival at the army conscript barracks in outer London. First, the clerk had asked for the letter that had been sent to him, notifying him of his call-up. Billy produced the letter, which had originally gone to Sheldon. The clerk glanced at it and put it to one side. Taking his identity card and ration book, the clerk told him the army would be issuing him with a new card and he wouldn't need the ration book. That all made sense to Billy. What was really puzzling him was what on earth had happened to Robby.

No sign of him when they were being fitted out with their kit; again no sign of him at the evening meal. And Robby had said that although he would be reporting independently – he had to go and say goodbye to an old aunt on the way – he would look out for him once he arrived.

When time came for lights out, Robby certainly wasn't in *Billy's* hut. Perhaps he was in another one, though Billy had noticed that whether it was a question of forming up, eating or sleeping, everything seemed to be done alphabetically, and in that respect their two surnames could not have been much closer.

The recruits were on the parade ground for three hours next morning. Hardly anyone had got his kit on right, or sufficiently right to satisfy the loud-mouthed sergeant-major. When at last that had been attended to, it was solid marching up and down, head up, chest out, swing the arms. Billy was so relieved at the end of it that he was not particularly perturbed when, after a young subaltern had come up and spoken a few words in his ear, the sergeant-major shouted out Billy's name and ordered him to stay behind. Perhaps they were going to tell him something about Robby.

But no, not immediately, it seemed. Instead the sergeant-major said, 'You're wanted in the duty room. Quick march and follow me.'

An orderly standing outside opened the door for them.

The sergeant-major came to attention noisily in front of an officer seated behind a table.

'New recruit Private Sexton reporting, sir,' he shouted out, and then, turning to his right, took two loud steps and turned to face the officer again.

'Ah, yes,' said the officer quietly, addressing the new recruit. 'Now, I presume your name *is* Sexton.'

'Yes,' replied Billy.

'Yes, *sir!*' shouted the sergeant-major.

'Yes, sir,' said Billy.

'Well, we seem to be in a bit of a muddle here,' said the officer. 'My pay corps people tell me we weren't expecting any recruit of that name. But the numbers are right. We weren't expecting you, but we're missing another recruit.'

'Is his name Sheldon?' asked Billy.

'Don't speak unless the officer tells you,' roared the sergeant-major.

'Yes, as a matter of fact, it is,' said the officer, ignoring the interruption. 'Do you know him?'

'Yes, sir,' said Billy.

'Well, you'll have to leave me to go into all this. Perhaps there was a mix-up with the call-up papers – I don't know what's happened. All right, you can fall out now. Carry on, sergeant-major.'

'*Sir!*' that worthy yelled, then bawled out orders to Billy to about turn, quick march, left, right, left, right...

Whenever Robby was in the pub near the theatre and Fay was there too, they joined up together. Occasionally they went to a Lyon's Corner House in Leicester Square and ate a plate of whatever modest food was on offer. He regularly spent the night on the divan in her room, particularly if he had a matinee the next day. They started to exchange a kiss at the end of an evening, but Fay never allowed the friendship to go beyond that.

Late one morning, after Fay had left for her

job in the cinema, he was still in the flat, lazing on the divan, reading a book he had brought with him. When he heard a knock, he got up, just wearing his underclothes, and opened the door.

'Oh, I was looking for Fay,' said the surprised caller. She was a large and lovely girl of about forty, with fair curly hair and enormous blue eyes, and a cheerful smile on her unmade-up face.

'Come in. I'm a friend, I've been staying the night here. Fay's gone off to work.'

'What d'you do about the key?' the caller asked inconsequentially. 'I mean, if you want to go out and Fay comes back?'

'We have a hiding place downstairs.'

'My name's Muriel.'

'Mine's Robby.'

They shook hands.

'Last time I saw her, she was on the evening shift.'

There was a pause. 'Afraid I can't offer you a drink,' said Robby.

'Don't worry, I've come prepared.'

Muriel proceeded to sit herself down in an armchair and produced a bottle of gin from a large handbag.

'Haven't got anything to go with it,' she said.

'There's always water,' said Robby.

Robby leant over her and gave her a firm kiss on the mouth. He had once seen a man do that in a film.

'Hey, that's a bit early for this,' Muriel said.

Robby went to get some water and some glasses.

'Why don't you take a few clothes off and make yourself more comfortable?' he said on his return.

After yet another rebuff from Fay, Robby had been feeling particularly frustrated that morning. For her part, it was many months since a man had shown any appreciation of Muriel and she was not going to pass up an encounter with a good-looking young man such as Robby. Robby's mistake was to urge this unknown stranger to visit him regularly and it was on one such occasion that he suffered a nasty blow to the head when Fay picked up a chair and crashed it down on him. She had felt unwell and returned early, long before the end of her shift. A scantily dressed Muriel had just returned from the bathroom along the corridor. Fay did not need any excuses or explanations, and grabbing the untidy mess of Muriel's clothes from the armchair, pushed her out of the room, throwing the clothes behind her.

'And now you get out too,' she yelled, 'and that's the last I ever want to see of you.'

Robby tried to remonstrate as he dressed hurriedly, but Fay went on shouting at him.

He never saw Fay again in the pub and he was nervous of going to call on her. In any event, his play was closing and he felt it was time to join the army. He had had a talk with the young author of the play at a party on the night it closed, who told him that he himself was about to report to the Army Kinematograph Service Corps. 'Helping write propaganda films,' he explained.

'But are you going direct to that, without any preliminary?' Robby asked.

'No, no,' was the reply. 'I've already done my basic army training – I'm *returning* to the corps. These last few months I've been on extended leave because of the play. My Colonel's been very good about it. I think the idea was to gain some prestige for the service with one of their number coming up with a literary sort of West End success. Keep the Ministry of Information off their backs!'

Robby reported to a west London recruiting office. On going through the form he had completed and seeing his date of birth, the elderly sergeant sitting opposite him said, 'Haven't you received a call-up order yet? You should have had one three months ago.'

'Yes, I did receive one and even went for a medical.' Then, lying, Robby went on, 'But I've never heard another word since.'

'I'll have to look into this,' replied the sergeant, looking at him suspiciously. 'Come back in a few days time.'

When Robby returned it was to hear that the

military police were looking for him. Had he changed his address? Robby answered yes. Why hadn't he notified the army authority? All mail was supposedly being sent on, said Robby.

'I heard nothing – that's why I'm here now.'

'Were you living at the same address as someone called Sexton?'

'Yes.'

'Well, your friend Sexton has since been discharged. Sounds a rum sort of bloke from what I read here,' observed the sergeant, looking down at a report in front of him. 'Should never have been called up in the first place – mentally unstable. Let's see your identity card.'

Robby produced it.

'Well, I suppose if you'd been trying to avoid service, you wouldn't be here now and I'm going to push your application through. We won't trust the post this time. I'm going to write it down for you; where to enlist and on what day and time. I'm putting on my report 'original enrolment order presumed destroyed by enemy action.'

The truth was the sergeant found the whole story unconvincing, but he had had few volunteers through his hands the last few weeks and felt it was about time he signed somebody up.

The instruction was for Robby to report to an infantry regiment. It was late October of 1944. The Second Front had been launched the previous

June and Allied armies were now meeting stiff resistance as they began pushing into Germany itself. In September the operation to secure the Rhine crossing at Arnhem had been abandoned. It did not look as if the war would be over by Christmas after all. For the British, five years of war had created a manpower crisis, especially in the infantry, and there was no talk of another medical for Robby. Nor were there any further questions about his delayed appearance. He was put straight into training.

The days were a round of roll-calls, parade-ground drills, battle drills, rifle practice and kit inspections. One day somebody decided that Robby was potential officer material.

At his selection board interview, he was asked if he had any preference as to the arm he wished to serve in.

Robby had not anticipated a question of this nature. He assumed he would be staying in the infantry. Suddenly he remembered his conversation with the young playwright.

'Ideally,' he said, as though in a dream, 'I should like to serve in the Army Kinematograph Service.'

The three offficers across the table stared at him speechless.

'I am by profession an actor and stage manager and feel, with my experience, I could be more useful there than in a combat regiment.'

Robby was amazed at his own daring, but continued to sit on his chair motionless.

At length the senior officer on the three man board, looking down at some papers before him, said, 'Hum, I see you show that as your civilian occupation. We will need to think about it. I don't know whether they require anyone at the moment.'

He was told to fall out and carry on with normal duties.

Afterwards, the playwright, whose duties then seemed to have become more clerical than artistic, used to tell Robby it was he who had spotted the application and recommended its acceptance to the Colonel. Whether the Colonel attached particular importance to the opinion of his young lieutenant is a matter of conjecture, but he was certainly not beyond indulging in empire building. So, after two weeks of officer training at another camp, where Robby was eventually passed out as a second lieutenant, he was told to report for duty to the chosen unit.

Temporary headquarters were on the coast of Scotland. A film was being made on a nearby beach. Robby, in his brand new officer's uniform, now somewhat creased after the long train journey, was immediately cast as a staff captain and the necessary change made to his epaulettes. Only after the day's shooting was over was he reunited with his kitbag and shown to his room in a hotel, one of several that had been commandeered. In the mess that night he met the Colonel, a peacetime film producer, who greeted him affably.

'Haven't quite thought how we're going to make full use of you yet,' the Colonel said, 'but report down to the set again tomorrow.'

Robby asked about his friend, the playwright.

'Back in London now,' said the Colonel, 'writing a film about tank production.'

By the end of March 1945, after Robby had been in Scotland for about six weeks, the film was completed. Actors, crew, the whole organisation returned to London. Soldiers on loan from the army returned to their units and the little coastal town settled once more into its winter desolation. Robby had continued to play the film role allotted to him on arrival, involving fewer and fewer appearances, but was kept busy assisting the director in placing the leading participants before camera and running messages to the far-flung groups of soldiers. However, he was glad to leave the bleak weather and baleful surroundings behind him. Some days had indeed been very unpleasant and on four days they had been unable to film because of snowfall.

The playwright's film about tank production was never made. The completed Scottish one was shelved, but taken over a year later by an independent producer and extended and given a proper plot, with a starring role for a well-known Hollywood-based British actor. Back in London, the Colonel regretfully informed Robby he had no more use for him. The war was virtually over and no more propaganda films were scheduled; the 'Kine Corps' was winding up. He would have to go back to his regiment.

Unfortunately Robby's original regiment was not prepared to recognise him as an infantry second lieutenant. He had gone straight from the officers' training school to the Kinematograph Service. He reported to the pool of unemployed officers.

No regiment applied for Robby's services. He was supernumerary, and after two months of idleness, he was discharged. Then he found that with more experienced hands now available, nobody wanted his services in the West End theatre. His efforts to break into provincial repertory tours, in whatever capacity, were likewise unsuccessful. Disillusioned, he answered a BBC advertisement in *The Stage* for production assistants. He went by appointment to Portland Place to be told all the jobs had since been filled. But, added the masculine-looking lady interviewing him – seeing Robby's look of dejection – why not try the television arm? After a perfunctory one-channel start in the thirties, this offshoot, after five years of silence, was about to start up again. She gave him the address to go to and a note to the staff manager.

'I dont know why you've been sent here,' said the staff manager. 'We're nothing like ready to put programmes on the air again. We don't need anybody at the moment. As it is, when we *do* start, it'll be only for short evenings and mainly news broadcasts.'

The bespectacled, middle-aged manager was a kindly man, and taking another look at Robby's handsome features, suddenly had an idea.

'I'm going to send you to see someone else,' he said, picking up an internal telephone.

Robby went to another office, where a trim, grey-haired man politely rose on Robby's entrance. They shook hands and he told Robby to sit down. After asking him a few questions, the man said, 'Come with me, I want you to do a test.'

Robby was installed in a soundproof booth.

'These are yesterday's news bulletins,' the man said, pointing to a board. 'You've been on the stage. Look straight at the camera in front of you in a friendly manner. Read what you see in a natural, relaxed way, at the right speed – not too fast, not too slow. Like you've heard news announcers on the wireless.'

After about five minutes, he was told to stop.

'I've been watching you on the screen. You look good, you've got the right inflection in your voice, anything else we can fix. You've done well!'

Since leaving the army, this was the first time

anyone had shown any interest in Robby, let alone of a complimentary nature, and he beamed with pleasure.

It was a bit of a let-down when the man said, 'Of course, we have already got a lead male announcer, but I can offer you the job of his relief. You'd be appearing several times a week.'

The pay wasn't much, but he could report the following Monday and generally make himself useful until actual broadcasts started. Robby felt it was a beginning.

The BBC's television service duly started up again. True, no new television sets were in the shops and only a few people had them from pre-war days. Knobs had to be twiddled to obliterate what looked like snowstorms in the studio or to sharpen up the wishy-washy picture. But Robby's occasional appearances became known to the small core of viewers, and his public grew as sets came on the market.

He was leaving the building one evening when somebody came up to him outside. It was Sexton.

'How are you, my dear fellow?' Robby stammered, after conquering his amazement.

Sexton had a wild look about him and was breathing heavily.

'It was thanks to you I had that terrible time in the army,' he spluttered without preamble. 'I should never have been called up. They found out someone had altered my letter. I've been looking for you for a long time.'

So saying, he took a fierce swipe at Robby. Robby ducked and hit back at him. Sexton toppled over, hitting his head hard on the pavement. He was unconscious and Robby could not rouse him. Blood was oozing from the side of his head. Robby went back into the studio and dialled for an ambulance.

While he was waiting outside for it to come – a still unconscious Sexton prone on the ground – a strolling policeman on his beat approached.

''Ullo, what have we got here? You two been fighting?'

'An unprovoked assault, officer. Never seen the man before.'

'You one of those blokes from the TV in there?'

'Yes.'

A few minutes later, Sexton was bundled into an ambulance.

'Probably have some identification on him,' remarked the policeman, wishing Robby a respectful good-night.

The fact that his old fellow-lodger in Chiswick had discovered his whereabouts awakened Robby's anxieties about the way his life was going. He still harboured the ambition to become an actor. Pleased as he was to get his job in the first place, he realised it was getting him nowhere. The main male announcer had become a household name and was showing no signs of abdicating any of his slots. To make matters worse, the BBC had hired a female announcer to cover programme links and on two occasions she had even been allowed to read the news. It was time to move on. His pay had been considerably increased since the day he joined and he had been saving money each week – enough to tide him over for a month or two anyhow. He would leave as soon as he could and meanwhile keep a good look out for the possible return of Sexton.

Sexton did not return, and the BBC were very decent about his leaving. In fact, they gave a small party on his last night.

One lunchtime Robby drifted into the pub in the heart of theatreland, which he used to frequent before he joined the army. He hadn't been inside it since. He was hoping to run into someone he knew from those earlier days, an actor or even a producer or agent perhaps, who might be able to help him get his foot on the ladder. He had already been to see the producer of the only play he had been involved in nearly three years previously, but the man had not been help-ful. On going up to the bar, he noticed two girls looking at him and giggling. He recognised Muriel first – the fat girl with whom he had had the affair in Fay's flat. Beside her was Fay herself, with, to his surprise, a friendly smile on her face.

As he approached them, it was Muriel who spoke first. 'We've seen you on the TV,' she said.

'So you two are friends again,' said Robby.

'We've always been friends,' said Fay firmly.

Robby bought them each a drink and one for himself. They went to a table and he started telling them about his life since he had last seen them. They did not know he had left the television.

'I'm trying to get back into the theatre. Do either of you know anyone who could help me?'

'Now that you're a famous face, it shouldn't be all that difficult,' answered Fay, waving at a middle-aged man who had just walked into the pub.

He came over when he had bought his drink and asked if he could join them. He was an actor, about to begin a tour of the provinces. He gave Robby the name of the production company that was putting on the tour.

Robby made a call on the company. Their offices comprised two small rooms at the top of an old building in St Martin's Lane. The boss was out, but a young man about his own age received him affably. The young man did not recognise him as the TV newsreader, but liked his looks and suggested he should come back again later, when the boss had returned. He made a careful note of the play in which Robby had appeared and where he also acted as assistant stage-manager, and wrote down what he had been doing since.

When Robby returned, he was told they were arranging another tour – starting in one month's time – of a play called *Gaslight Shadows*, and he was given extracts of a possible part to read aloud. Both the boss and the young man seemed pleased and told him to report for rehearsals the following week. The role was a subsidiary one, but contained several strong scenes, where the actor was bound to be noticed. The pay was not particularly attractive, but the firm would be looking after the lodging in the various towns and the cost of all transport, so he would only have to find his food. Had he got some respectable clothes? They wanted to keep down the cost of hiring from costumiers. Had he got a dinner-jacket? He still had the suit the BBC had bought for him to read the news in the evenings. The boss seemed relieved he wouldn't have to be hiring that.

It was the third week of the tour and the company was playing in Northampton. Business was good and the theatre was almost full. Robby had just finished the scene where he was alone on the stage with the heroine, ending with her exiting left. He was now all alone, looking suitably shattered and moving around the stage silently, before the moment when the curtain came down to bring the first act to a close. Suddenly he noticed a man trying to scramble on to the side of the stage. Robby gazed in horror as the man got himself up and advanced towards him. He was holding a knife and lunged wildly at Robby. Robby dodged the knife and hurled the assailant into what used to be the orchestra pit, but which had been converted during the war into three extra rows of stalls. The man ended up face downwards on some hard wooden flooring, narrowly missing the people in the front row, by then on their feet and doing their best to keep out of the way. The curtain was rung down, as it happened pretty much on cue, but the effect, although dramatic enough, was hardly as the playwright intended.

The show went on, after a long interval. Police and ambulance men were called. The man was carried out. Backstage, the cast were told he was dead. Robby knew the attacker was his old nemesis, Sexton. He must have come to see the play before; he must have waited for this particular moment when Robby would be alone. But what he was doing in Northampton, and how he found out about the play and Robby's appearance in it, he never fathomed. One thing seemed clear, however: poor old Billy Sexton had been intent on harming his old Chiswick friend in the most public and attention-seeking manner possible. The next day Robby was questioned by the police, but could give no reason for the attack. There would be an inquest, of course, he was told.

The Northampton 'stringer' for the *Daily Mirror*, who had been sent a free ticket, was in the audience that night. It was many years since he had had anything interesting like this to send in to the paper. It hadn't been for want of trying, but whatever items he submitted never seemed to warrant publication. There was nothing in the programme about Robby being an ex-TV announcer, but – funny – when he had been watching Robby on stage, he was sure he had seen him somewhere. And when he went round to interview him at the end of the play, Robby was able to answer the question: he used to be on the television! So late that night, too late for the next day's paper, but it didn't matter, the stringer was able to phone in the full story. He even added a conjecture about a grievance the would-be killer had been harbouring, something dating back several years, perhaps to Robby's army days, when Robby had been fighting valiantly for his country...

When the *Mirror* broke the news, it was the second lead on the front page, with a picture and back-up story over two pages inside.

'Corky' Cochrane was only a small London-based theatrical agent at the time. In fact, since starting on his own, after being demobbed from the navy,

97

he hadn't really had very much to show for his efforts. Did Robby Sheldon have an agent, he wondered? He knew him as a good-looking young fellow from the TV, but the answer was probably not, or he wouldn't – with his familiar face – be stuck in some second-rate repertory set-up. He was down to Northampton the same day he saw the story. He hung around outside the stage door and buttonholed Robby when he arrived for the evening performance. He explained he was an agent, and Robby agreed to meet him for a drink after the show.

They went to a pub. 'When the tour's over, I want you to come and see me,' said Corky, handing Robby his card. 'I enjoyed the play and in my view you stood out.'

Robby murmured his thanks.

'I'd seen you on TV and recognised your name, of course, when I read the paper this morning, but I'd no idea you'd left the BBC. In fact, that nasty incident last night is the sole reason I'm here.'

Corky had come to Northampton to sign up what he expected to be a fairly ordinary sort of actor, but was beginning to sense he might have found a star.

'For how many more weeks is the tour going on?'

Before Robby could answer, the publican called 'time'.

Someone in the pub told them of a drinking

club that was open till eleven thirty. There was a lot of talk about membership at the door, but a pound note from Corky fixed that technicality.

The tour had another five weeks to go. Corky assured him he wouldn't be idle for long after it had finished. 'And don't go talking to anyone else in the meantime,' he added.

Before the war, Corky had worked for a big theatrical agency and could still open most doors. Nevertheless it took rather longer than he anticipated to get Robby, or Robert – as he was to become under the new aegis – established. Small parts in films, in the odd TV play coming into production... But his face, his speaking voice and his effortless handling of different roles were being noticed by people who mattered. When the producers of the first 'musketeer' film were looking for a relative newcomer to fill the starring role, he was on the shortlist.

'And to think I would never have come down to see you and signed you up if I hadn't read about the trouble you had with that madman on stage,' Corky never tired of repeating over the years. If Robby had a conscience, he didn't allow it to trouble him.

'You need a bit of luck in life,' he always replied.

Russian Approach

It was half-way through a round of golf at Sunningdale that Clive Hammond came out with his strange proposition. Though doubtless not his intention, it put me off my game and he ended up beating me. I have lost count of the number of times that, for some reason or another, I have been sure that I have finally got the game licked. I have discovered some new little thing, which seemed to be the key to the game's mastery, only to drift back into my old erratic ways. This was one of the days, however, when all was going well and I felt on top of the world.

We were walking down the fairway of the long seventh hole, having driven off, when he asked me whether I might be interested in helping finance a project that could end up making millions. I murmured a not uninterested reply and he started to tell me how he had got friendly with a key employee in the Russian Government, who was keen to become involved with the massive privatisation of state assets currently under way. His friend's particular opportunity involved Russian embassies abroad. (I should add at this juncture that the conversation I am writing about took place some years ago, before Vladimir Putin became President.) As Clive started to go into more details, I suggested that we resume discussion once back in the clubhouse, but I found it difficult to keep the subject out of my mind.

I was staggered when it became clear over lunch that the embassy under discussion was the Russian embassy in London, the huge freehold building on the corner of Kensington Palace Gardens and Bayswater Road, standing in almost two acres of grounds. Once acquired from the government and in private hands, Clive envisaged its demolition and a development into a tall building of offices and flats, with a range of shops underneath. It would not be the idea to do the development ourselves, he said, but to sell the scheme to a major English property company.

'If my friend and his associates can buy the site at anything like the knock-down prices the state oil companies are going for,' he went on, 'the difference against London market value will be enormous.'

Before negotiating a price, however, those at the Russian end needed financial backing, which in effect meant a commitment from a bank, which in turn meant a consortium of investors putting up a hefty sum of cash in order to obtain the loan. Russian banks were out; there were too few to choose from and even discussing the deal with one of them could spur a rival offer from either the bank itself or close associates of theirs. A foreign bank was the only way to preserve a clear playing-field.

I readily saw the sense of this, but was still mystified how government officials could themselves put up an offer.

'They will act purely as agents on behalf of English investors and present the offer as the best available ... and, more importantly, recommend it,' Clive said. 'After all, the government itself has made clear its interest in selling overseas assets along with its domestic ones.'

'How important is your friend?' was my next question. 'I imagine he would have to have the ear of the ultimate person responsible for agreeing the sale.'

'He is the number two in the Ministry of State Education.'

'Doesn't sound very promising to me!' I expostulated.

'I happened to meet him at a diplomatic reception in London a few months ago,' Clive said, ignoring my remark. 'He was over here on some educational research business. He asked me what I did and when I said I was in the property business, his ears pricked up. We got on well and we had a dinner together before he went back to Moscow. It turned out his brother is the chairman of the government-appointed privatisation committee. Things rather developed from there.'

'So presumably he and his brother will expect a handsome stake in whatever company is formed over here to bid for the building.'

'Very much so. And there may be others who will have to be accommodated – I don't know. People even higher up.'

'But what's the lowest stake you would agree to for you and your financial backers?'

'Rather depends on the price my Russian friends end up paying, but I wouldn't want to go below fifty per cent.'

It was some three weeks before Clive Hammond contacted me again. 'My man is coming to London again next week,' he said. 'I want you to meet him.' He went on to give me a proposed time and place.

Clive had taken a private room at the Oxford and Cambridge Club in Pall Mall and we were both sitting there on the agreed evening at six o'clock when a club servant showed in the Russian. Clive gave the visitor an effusive greeting and then introduced him to me. I found myself looking at a small, trim individual in his mid-thirties, with rimless spectacles and wearing a dark suit and tie. His name was Dmitri Yogosoff.

After giving me a brief bow, Mr Yogosoff crossed to a long piece of furniture on one side of the room, where he had apparently noticed a telephone. Seizing it and turning it upside down, he scrutinised the base carefully. Then, getting on his knees at one side of the table in the centre of the room, he spent several moments looking underneath. The centre light, an art deco affair, and other objects in the room were being given a cursory look-over when Clive said, 'Dmitri, this is a private club. Nobody's eavesdropping – you have nothing to fear.'

Dmitri's body became less taut and he gave a thin smile.

So far, on this particular visit, Clive and the Russian had only spoken briefly on the telephone, and this evening was their first actual meeting. 'Are you any further on?' Clive asked him, obviously referring to the matter they had discussed during their one dinner together.

'An acceptable price to the government would be the market value of the property on the basis of no permission for redevelopment,' Yogosoff said in slow, careful English.

'And what do you reckon that price would be?'

'Five million pounds.'

'I'll have to round up some more investors, apart from my friend here,' said Clive calmly, looking at me, 'but at that price, I should think you've got a deal.'

There was a silence and I decided to come into the conversation myself. 'Dmitri here,' I said to Clive, 'is going to be in on our end of things too, so let's get down to basics. OK, you and I get some more people in to secure the bank loan, but what's their worst case scenario? If whoever you have in mind to sell to can't get planning permission to develop, they'll back away and we're stuck with it.'

It was Dmitri who answered. His exaggerated behaviour on arrival had irritated me, but he now spoke quietly and authoritatively: 'There's no reason why it shouldn't fetch double that for sale as a private house...'

'Or,' broke in Clive, 'the council could hardly refuse a request to convert the building into flats. Either way we'd cover the investment and bank interest.'

It wasn't long before the two of them, convinced of the need for a development on that particular corner of London and the unlikelihood of the council's planning department thinking otherwise, were discussing floors best allotted for offices and the whereabouts and number of flats. An American-style shopping complex over the ground and mezzanine floors, with its own level of underground car-parking space, would also be applied for.

When Clive started expounding on the amount of money professional developers could make out of the scheme, and indirectly what they might be prepared to pay the syndicate, I thought it was time for me to go. Such day-dreaming struck me as premature, with so many hurdles still to jump.

On noticing me rising, Yogosoff said, 'Are you not going to be with us for the rest of the evening?' I shook my head. 'In that case, I must put a point to you before you leave – something I should like you both to hear together.'

I sat down again as Yogosoff continued. 'I am in an awkward position at the present time as regards money. For instance, this visit to London I am making now, I have had to pay for myself. I had no reason to come over on Ministry business and I am taking the time as part of my annual leave. Even booking a holiday ticket abroad is not something that can be kept secret for long in Moscow and I had to inform my minister of my reasons. He did not object, but he is another person who will expect a share in your proposed consortium. If I have to spend more time away, he may even expect some immediate money to compensate for the loss of my services, or that is how he will doubtless put it. My brother on the privatisation committee may also feel he needs some immediate inducement to assure him of your good intentions. Government employees in our country are not well paid; in fact they are always short of money, but they have standards to keep up and like to feel they are doing the best for their children, sending them to fee-paying schools for example...'

He stopped talking and I couldn't help asking him how he obtained such an excellent command of English. 'I was an interpreter,' he replied. 'My knowledge of English got me my job in the Ministry of State Education and helped me rise to the top, permanent secretary I think you would call it over here.'

Clive frowned at me for my irrelevant interruption. 'What you are saying, Dmitri, is you need cash upfront ... now. What sort of money are you thinking of?'

'Fifty thousand pounds – in cash.'

'But that is an enormous amount. I quite see you have people to keep sweet on your side, but it's asking us to take a lot on trust. What happens if you can't deliver, can't give us the chance to buy the embassy at the price you have mentioned?'

'I couldn't guarantee to repay it.'

'This certainly needs a lot of thinking over,' Clive remarked. After a pause, he went on, 'I think we'll now go and have dinner. Perhaps we can reach some sort of compromise. Sure you won't join us?' he asked me.

'Sorry, I didn't know that was the plan. I have a dinner engagement,' I said truthfully.

That night Clive agreed with Yogosoff to pay him an initial £25,000, which the Russian would take back with him in cash. There would be no difficulty with customs at Moscow airport, Yogosoff informed him, as production of his ministerial pass entitled him to avoid all formalities. He would change the money into roubles on the black market – at a better rate than could be obtained at a bank, he had laughed.

Clive had been uneasy giving Yogosoff even half what he wanted, but had done so on the understanding Yogosoff would receive him in Moscow the following week and introduce him to the minister of his department and also to his brother chairing the privatisation committee.

'I'll get a clearer picture once I'm there,' Clive told me. 'The worst that can happen is I lose twenty five thousand pounds and the cost of the air ticket. But hopefully I'll come back satisfied that everything is as he says it is. Apart from anything else, I'll want to make sure they have access to the title deeds.'

To my relief there was no suggestion that I should contribute to these commitments, although Clive went out of his way to stress to me that he was only a small-time property dealer – a fact that I knew – and that he had limited funds behind him. Meanwhile Yogosoff was arranging to take him to the Embassy in London on some pretext or other, so he could see the size of the building and the area of ground it stood on.

Ten days later, when Clive returned from Moscow, he was in ebullient mood; he told me of his meetings at the Education Ministry and in the offices of the brother's committee and said he was satisfied with everybody's credentials.

'Even the famous brother will have to get the

deal nodded through by *somebody*,' I remarked. 'Have you thought of that?'

'Yes,' Clive answered. 'Probably the President's number two or at any rate one of the three or four key people who surround him – they're all ex-KGB or old friends or both. Evidently the President himself is often "very tired" – a euphemism, from what I've read – and leaves more and more decisions to his circle.'

'Some more people to have to look after,' I said.

'Yes, it's certainly turning out more complicated than I expected.'

Clive was acquainted slightly with two brothers who lived in Norfolk and who had become rich running a massive fish-marketing operation. He arranged to go and see them and insisted I should accompany him.

Horace and Bill Cleethorpe were both bachelors, living in some style in the village of Camborne Minster outside Ipswich. When Clive had told them he wanted to come and discuss a business proposition, they had not demurred and suggested we came to their house late one afternoon. We drew up outside some closed iron gates, behind which we could see a large Tudor house. The gates opened after we had spoken into the intercom and we drew up outside an ancient wooden front door at the top of some steps. We were getting out of the car when a large, florid man, who turned out to be Horace, came down the steps to meet us.

We walked into a high-domed hall and crossed to the far end, where the other brother, Bill, was standing beside a roaring fire. Horace started pouring out whiskies, and eventually we all sat down on two sofas facing each other in the middle of the hall. I noticed that each brother had a pad of paper and pencil lying beside him.

Clive launched into a detailed history of the opportunity that had come his way, starting with his first meeting with Yogosoff and omitting nothing. When he had finished, Horace said, 'So I suppose you need us for the financing stage ... when you have to find say half a million to comfort the bank giving you the loan.'

'I can't do the deal unless I have that sort of backing,' Clive said. 'I don't have anything like that money myself, nor has my friend.'

'Well, what's the deal *for us*? What do we get out of it?'

'One way and another, I can't see the Russians accepting less than a fifty per cent share of the syndicate, so that leaves fifty per cent for the English end.'

'We wouldn't be looking to finance any of your, shall we say, expenses incurred to date or in the future,' remarked a hitherto-silent Bill.

'How do you mean "in the future"? There's only the other half of Yogosoff's fifty thousand, which I can manage myself.'

'Don't worry, they'll be back for more,' Bill concluded.

'We'll have to think about it and let you know,' said Horace, getting up to top up our glasses from the whiskey decanter. 'I can't see us agreeing to have less than half of whatever you manage to salvage for the English side.'

'But I'm not asking you to take any risk,' exclaimed Clive. 'You supply the money for the bank and they won't release this or their own financing until the day the contract for sale of the property is signed.'

'Without our money, there's no contract,' observed Bill morosely.

Neither brother, either then or in the future, made any query about the price the Russians were asking. As Clive started to expound on the considerable upturn that could be expected once planning permission had been obtained, Horace got to his feet, grabbing his pad of paper and pencil, and asked to be excused for a few minutes.

He went and sat at a flat-topped desk away from where we were sitting and we all became silent. I sat sipping my whiskey and did not look at Clive. When Horace returned to join us, he said, 'Thank you, I have done my own calculations. I am satisfied as regards upturn.' After a pause, he went on, 'Bill, if you are agreeable, I suggest these two gentlemen come and see us again ... when they have got a little further along the road.'

Bill nodded.

'Does that mean we can count on you?' said Clive. 'It may not be long before I get to the stage when I have to commit. And the Russians won't commit themselves without seeing evidence from a bank that I have the funds.'

'I just feel you have a little way to go before you will wish to commit, on behalf of yourself and any backers,' Horace said obtusely.

We were unable to persuade the brothers to meet us any further, and with handshakes all round, we soon departed.

Unfortunately neither of us could think of any other substantial entrepreneurs to approach, without risking their wanting to take over the deal for themselves and our becoming little more than commission agents. Clive understandably became dejected and I was wishing I had never got involved in the affair. The potential amount of money to be made was, of course, tempting, but I had got my own affairs to think about as well. In fact, soon after the meeting in Norfolk, I took off for South America, where I had urgent business. On my return, I was surprised to find that Clive had been to Moscow again, and, incidentally, been obliged to commit to yet more cash, as Bill Cleethorpe had predicted. However, this time he had obtained a formal 'letter of intent'. He was now waiting for Yogosoff to come to England with a translation of the deed of contract, which Clive could show to a firm of international lawyers. Then, after an architect had checked the site for measurements and the lawyers had established proof of title to freehold, the deal would be ready to go ahead. But still subject to the little matter of basic financing...

The Cleethorpe brothers were still stalling. Clive went to see them again, this time on his own, and having agreed to give them, without further argument, a twenty five per cent share of the London consortium, came away with their written agreement to put up the amount of money the bank would require, subject to a limit of ten per cent of purchase price.

Eventually Yogosoff reappeared with the deed of contract, prepared in two languages. Clive had already obtained an agreement with an American bank in principle, but first he planned to take Yogosoff to his solicitors. The three of us were again in the meeting room at Clive's club.

'Exactly who is the bank to make the draft out to?' Clive queried, giving the contract a quick glance. 'I see it is left blank here.'

'On that I am still awaiting instructions,' the Russian replied.

It must have been the months of exasperation and dogged endurance of Yogosoff's generally devious behaviour that suddenly caused Clive to explode.

'Look here, Dmitri, I don't know what you and your friends are playing at, but I'm just beginning

114

to wonder whether I want to have anything further to do with this deal.'

Dmitri looked at him stony-faced.

'In fact, I think I'm going to walk away from the whole thing. You've now extracted from me well over the fifty thousand pounds you originally requested and what goodwill am I getting in return? As far as I'm concerned you lot can keep all the money...'

'You have not got much choice,' Yogosoff murmured.

'I've lost all trust in you,' Clive continued heatedly. 'Go and sell your deal somewhere else.'

Yogosoff was not going to let Clive off lightly. 'It happens that on my last trip I met Lord Lewinstein,' he said.

Both Clive and I recognised the name of the chairman of a publicly-quoted property company, a stout, dapper Labour Party supporter.

'Believe me, it was quite casual – at an embassy reception.'

'Another?' said Clive, thinking of their own first meeting.

'Yes, they are held quite frequently. This time it was in honour of the President of Nigeria.'

'Your deal sounds up his street. I hope he was interested.'

'Our talk was very brief, but as an experienced property man he quickly perceived the opportunities arising out of what I have been instructed to arrange. He foresaw an eventual multi-million pound flotation, embracing many of our embassies throughout the world.'

I could see Clive's rage building up further. Usually a composed, cheerful, not easily roused individual, his face had turned red.

Yogosoff spoke again: 'I am naturally sorry you have decided to withdraw. You will please return to me the letter of intent you received.'

'Tell your new friend to come and get it!' Clive shouted. 'Now get out. It is unnecessary for us to meet again.'

When I read in the papers a few days later of the death of a visiting Russian politician – his name was not given – in an accident at a crowded tube station, where he had apparently fallen on the line in front of an oncoming train, I wondered if the man could have been Dmitri Yogosoff. I telephoned Clive, but neither on that occasion nor the next day was I able to obtain a reply. I was getting worried when I received an un-expected telephone call from Horace Cleethorpe, who announced that he had been trying likewise to find my friend. Not having any success, he was coming to London the next day to see *me*. 'Did you read about the Russian getting killed by the train? Is it your man?' he asked in an agitated manner. I replied truthfully I did not know.

I remembered I had given Horace my card the day Clive and I went to visit him and his brother.

He told me he would be at my office at eleven o'clock and if I could find Clive in the meantime to ensure he was there too.

Horace duly arrived, clad in a tweed suit of greenish hue, and embarked on a list of complaints and worries. After I had calmed him down, I saw that basically all he and his brother wanted was to withdraw their backing for the embassy deal.

'It's all off anyhow,' I told him. Clive evidently had not notified him of the fact. 'You won't be asked to put up any money.'

'I don't want my name and my brother's becoming public if the man under the train turns out to be your contact and the police start delving too much,' Horace continued heatedly.

'There's no fear of that,' I assured him. 'The only people who know your names are our bank. The Russians were never told about you.'

'Well, my brother and I gave Clive Hammond a signed bit of paper agreeing to put up the money the bank would require – I want that back.'

'Alas,' I said, 'there's only one person who can give you that.' We rang Clive's number, but again getting no reply, we agreed to go round in person.

We took a taxi to the block of flats in Lowndes Square, where Clive lived and also had his office. We rang his bell and banged on the door, to no effect. Eventually we dug out a porter, who informed us that he hadn't seen Mr Hammond for some days. He did not know whether he was still sleeping there or whether he had – to use his words – gone off on one of his trips.

Horace and I went to have a drink at the nearby Berkeley Hotel. Horace was still worried about the letter Clive had been given and I kept assuring him that it was valueless without the accompanying cash advance. He left me with my promise to let him know when I found my friend.

The next morning I received a letter from Clive through the post. Strangely, it was postmarked some days earlier. It consisted of two pages of rambling typescript.

I have made myself ill, worrying about the situation I have got myself into. The Russians have pretty well cleaned me out of cash and I am at my overdraft limit. I was counting so much on the deal going through. Was I hasty, irrational if you like, in calling it off? I just knew I could not trust them any longer. Now they have fallen out amongst themselves or so Dmitri tells me. He says he's in danger and wants to see me again, but I refused. I don't know what's going to happen now, I just feel like going to sleep forever. Thank you sincerely for all the support you gave me, old friend. I'm so glad I didn't cost you any money...

I didn't like the sound of this letter. I determined to get into his flat. It took a lot of persuasion to convince the porter, and a fifty pound note, to give me his duplicate keys. I opened the door.

The whole place had been ransacked. Drawers and filing cabinets had been forcibly opened, their contents strewn over the floor. I noticed a dried pool of blood by the kitchen door. Beyond lay my friend, Clive Hammond, dead. A revolver was on the floor beside him.

I touched nothing, locked the flat up and put the keys in my pocket. Luckily I did not see the porter on the way out. I took a taxi straight to Gerald Road police station.

A detective-inspector accompanied me on a journey back again. I explained how I had been worried about the dead man, not having been able to make contact with him, and had obtained entry into his flat. I said nothing about the letter I had received, nor about our negotiations with Dmitri Yogosoff. Soon the flat was full of police photographers and fingerprint men. I was held at the police station and questioned for over an hour.

Who did it? The verdict at the inquest was death caused by person or persons unknown, or suicide. Knowing Clive, I was sure the latter was unlikely, and, in any event, why should he have made such a mess of his flat? However, the court was told that he was in financial difficulties and his mind may have been disturbed. His files and papers had been studied, but nothing that could incriminate a business associate or rival was discovered. He had been dead for some days. There were two lots of blurred fingerprints on the gun, one of them Clive's.

119

You may ask why I didn't tell the police about the Russians and my own suspicions. The famous letter of intent Clive had obtained from Yogosoff was obviously not found. Nor was Horace's letter mentioned, so that was missing too. But who could the police have gone to? The embassy would, probably rightly, claim to know nothing, and British policemen would get nowhere trying to interview a whole lot of people in Moscow. And yet, if I had spoken up, perhaps I could at least have cleared my friend of the imputation of suicide. Looking back, I suppose I just did not want to draw any attention to myself – it was as simple as that.

Taormina

Jonathan Powell was unpacking his case, having
been shown to his room at the Grand Hotel
Michelangelo in Taormina on the island of Sicily.
He opened the door of a big old-fashioned oak
wardrobe, almost as high as the ceiling, when a
man's body fell out.

Without ado, he went down to the concierge's
desk in the hall. A young, sleek-haired Italian was
on duty.

'There's a dead body in my room,' Jonathan
announced.

'What is your room number, sir?' the concierge
replied blandly.

'I-I'm not sure.'

'What is it you want, sir?'

'I don't really want anything. I've just come to
report a dead body.'

'One moment please, sir' said the concierge,
disappearing to an office behind his desk.

A few minutes later, an older man came out,
resplendent in a uniform of royal blue, with cross-

keys insignia on his lapels. Smiling, he asked, 'You have something you wish to report, sir? How can I help?'

The younger man stepped aside to attend to a hotel guest asking for postage stamps, while Jonathan embarked on a detailed explanation of what had befallen him. After a difficult conversation, the head concierge requested Jonathan to follow him across the hall to the check-in desk. He said something to the young girl on duty and told Jonathan to wait by the desk. Bowing, he then departed back to his own domain.

'I'll see if I can find the manager for you, sir,' the young girl said with a bright smile.

When the manager eventually appeared at Jonathan's side, he arrived with outstretched hand and asked Jonathan to accompany him to his office. Seated opposite the manager at his desk, Jonathan saw a man in his late forties, wearing narrow-rimmed spectacles and dressed in a black suit. Speaking perfect English, he said, 'Am I to understand there has been an accident in your room?'

'I don't know about an accident. A man's body fell out of my wardrobe, and from the quick look I had before coming down to report it, it looked more like murder. There was a bullet wound in the side of his head.'

The manager gave no sign of emotion or curiosity. 'We will both go to the police station and you must file a report.'

* * *

The hotel was at the bottom of a narrow side road off the town's main avenue. Half-way up the side road, Jonathan saw a sign 'POLIZIA' sticking out of a small two-storey building. They went inside and, addressing a uniformed policeman behind a glass grille, the manager asked to see the *Capo di Carabinieri*.

The policeman pushed a form towards him from under the grille, with a jocular remark.

The manager became angry. In Italian that Jonathan could understand, he was shouting: 'Not every guest who comes to my hotel is reporting the loss of his passport!'

When the Chief arrived, he shook hands with the manager and was then introduced to Jonathan. As the manager unfolded the story, the Chief began to eye Jonathan suspiciously. 'Did you touch anything?' he suddenly said to Jonathan in English.

'No. You will find everything exactly as I found it.'

Taormina is a sprawling town on a hill dating back to Grecian times, and highly popular with American, English, French and German tourists, often stopping for no more than a few days as part of a tour of Italy. Indeed, Jonathan was only there on a short springtime break from his job with a British oil company in Rome.

123

After walking back to the hotel with the manager, he found he had already been allotted another room and his belongings had been transferred. It was five o'clock and he lay on his bed, half expecting a visit from the management or the police, but there was no knock on the door. At seven o'clock he went downstairs to the bar, and, after making short work of a couple of dry martini cocktails, proceeded to the terrace restaurant. Neither the barman nor any other member of staff gave him a second look. Both in the bar and in the restaurant guests chatted among themselves in a normal fashion. The hotel's obviously keeping this incident very quiet, he thought.

After dinner, he decided to go for a walk in the town. As he went out, the young concierge to whom he had originally spoken called out a friendly *buona sera*. All the cafés in the main square were very crowded and he was obliged to ask a little old lady sitting at a table for four on her own whether he could take one of the places. They started talking and it transpired she was on holiday in the town by herself, in fact had been coming for some twenty years at this time of year. Perhaps it was the cocktails and the wine he had consumed at dinner, or because he felt so lonely and helpless, that he suddenly started confiding in her.

'It wouldn't be the first unexplained murder, or disappearance for that matter, that has happened on this island over the last few years,' the lady remarked in a matter-of-fact way.

Startled at both her knowledge and her lack of any surprise, Jonathan said, 'How do you know about such things?'

'Over the years I've made a lot of friends here – shopkeepers, waiters, all sorts of people. Often they tell me things.'

Jonathan waited for her to go on.

'I wonder whether the murder you are telling me about had something to do with an ongoing political feud,' she added thoughtfully. 'There are a lot of people on this island who were very devoted followers of Mussolini.'

'But that's all a long time ago. Italy's a democracy now.'

'Yes, but not everybody is particularly happy with the present government,' the lady went on. 'It's remarkable how the man in charge has been able to accumulate so much money and become so powerful, with all his stakes in industry, newspapers and television. Seems to be above the law too.

'Leave me to think about it and make some enquiries,' she ended. 'Where are you staying?'

It turned out they were staying at the same hotel. Excited, Jonathan urged her to have dinner with him the following night. They walked back together. Going down the main street, with shops still open on either side, with a little smile she led him into an old curio shop. Almost hidden at the back, she pointed out some small ebony busts of Mussolini. They started looking at other things when they noticed the shopkeeper watching them.

For their dinner together the next evening, they had arranged to meet first in the hall of the hotel. Jonathan gave his name formally and the lady introduced herself as Miss Heathcott. They were seated at a table on the terrace and had given their order when Miss Heathcott suddenly said, 'I've found out who the murdered man was.'

Jonathan, to whom neither the police nor anybody on the staff of the hotel had still spoken a word, spluttered out: 'How on earth did you do that?'

'I asked Bruno, the manager. He's an old friend.'

'And who was he?'

'His name doesn't matter, but he was a rich businessman from Palermo. He had been staying in the hotel on his own and had checked out that morning.'

'How did he get back into his room?'

'Perhaps he kept his passkey.'

'And why should he want to go back?'

'Perhaps the murderer got him back on some pretext. Told him he'd left something valuable behind.'

'Then the murderer would have to have been somebody working at the hotel.'

'That's what I have got to find out,' Miss Heathcott remarked pleasantly.

Try as he could, Jonathan was unable to draw her out further. She started to talk of Mount Etna, the volcano high on a mountain, which dominated the town, and which had evidently last erupted three years before when Miss Heathcott was staying at the hotel. 'None of the debris got anywhere near the town on that occasion,' she prattled on.

'What are the police doing about it all?' asked Jonathan, getting a word in towards the end of the meal.

'I understand two officers are coming over from Palermo tomorrow.'

The afternoon of the next day Jonathan noticed Miss Heathcott sitting in the hotel garden on a bench overlooking the bay.

'I always find it so peaceful here,' she said, 'looking at the sea and watching all the sailing boats go by.'

'Have you been able to find out anything more?' broke in Jonathan.

'Come and sit down. Yes, the police have told Bruno and Bruno's told me – in strict confidence of course – that the murdered gentleman was an active member of a group on the island seeking independence from Italy.'

'To make Sicily an independent republic?'

127

'Yes. There is a strong industrial economy here, you know, quite apart from the wine growing and tourism. It seems, however, that there is a certain amount of squabbling going on over the leadership between various factions. But one thing I have been able to discover this morning, not from Bruno incidentally, is that this strange movement is made up of die-hard followers of Mussolini, old devotees of the kind I mentioned when we first met.

'Bruno claims not to know the murdered man, but if he's who I think he is, from a description the floor maid was good enough to give me, I saw him in Taormina a few years ago, one night when I was dining at a restaurant and noticed the two of them together in a corner. Being naturally curious, I found out from the restaurant owner – I helped him start the place up; he used to be the wine waiter here – that they had known each other from boyhood, when their two fathers, both sadly shot by partisans towards the end of the war evidently, were leading lights in the Fascist party in Sicily and close to Mussolini himself.

'By the way, have the Palermo police interviewed you yet?' Miss Heathcott added.

'Yes. Not much I could tell them really. I just gave a short statement.'

'I think I will now take myself for my usual little walk, if you will excuse me,' Miss Heathcott concluded. 'Why don't we meet for a drink in the town before dinner?'

*　*　*

Seated in the bar she had suggested, on a first floor with a magnificent sea view, Jonathan quickly pointed out the owner of the curio shop which they had visited. He was sitting with a well-dressed middle-aged woman.

'Yes, I had noticed them,' said Miss Heathcott. 'That woman was staying at the hotel at the time I saw Bruno and his friend having dinner together. By the way, I never told you, I went into the curio shop again this morning and the Mussolini busts were gone. And when I asked whether I could buy one, the shopkeeper claimed he'd never had any!'

'You sound like a Scotland Yard detective on holiday,' laughed Jonathan.

Miss Heathcott looked pained.

Later, for the second evening running, they dined together, this time meeting at the table. Jonathan rose as Miss Heathcott arrived.

'I have just learnt of the most terrible thing,' she said softly, settling herself in her chair, 'and I was so hoping there wouldn't be a second murder.'

'Second murder? Who?'

'Poor Bruno, the manager!'

'Who told you?'

'Giovanni!'

129

'Who's Giovanni?'

'The head concierge. Been here for as long as I can remember.'

They broke off as the head waiter arrived to take their order. Jonathan asked him to wait while they both quickly scanned the menu.

'Evidently he was travelling along the coast road by the town little more than an hour ago when his car went out of control and crashed over the cliff. He was found dead in it down by the shore,' Miss Heathcott continued, after the waiter had gone.

'Could have been an accident,' murmured Jonathan.

'I have no doubt the incident will be brought in as such,' his companion replied.

They looked up to see the distinguished-looking woman they had noticed in the bar being shown to a table.

'So she's staying here,' Miss Heathcott remarked. 'Very interesting.'

After dinner, they found a quiet corner in the bridge room and sat down, asking a waiter to bring them coffee. At the other end of the room two games of bridge were going on. Speaking quietly, Miss Heathcott started explaining about the continuing influence of the Mafia in Sicilian politics. 'You don't want to fall foul of them,' she told Jonathan, 'and they have a way of usually being on the winning side. To what extent, if any, they're mixed up in all this, I have no idea. They're not above switching loyalties too. You may remember how at the height of Mussolini's power, in 1943, they collaborated with General Eisenhower – for rather a lot of money, I'm sure – to give considerable help to the Allied invasion of Sicily from North Africa.'

Jonathan was largely ignorant of Second World War history. 'Were they always against Mussolini, then?' he asked.

'Rather the contrary, I believe. He made a lot of noise but didn't interfere with them.'

'Have you planned your next move?' Jonathan was enjoying his friend's detective work.

'Oh, yes. Tomorrow I must become acquainted with that lady we have seen twice tonight.'

One of the bridge players turned round to frown at their murmurings and after a while they both retired to bed.

Jonathan slept late the next morning. When he was finally up and dressed, he decided to go and sit in the sun in the courtyard on the garden side of the hotel and read his day-old paper. He spotted the mysterious lady who was so much the object of Miss Heathcott's interest. She was sitting at a table on her own, with a pot of coffee in front of her. Chuckling to himself at this chance to upstage his friend with a piece of detective work

131

of his own, he went up to the table and asked if he might join her.

She looked at him with some surprise, but after explaining that he was an Englishman on a first visit and needing a bit of advice on what to see and do, she motioned to him to sit down.

He watched as she poured herself out another cup of coffee, waiting for him to start talking. She was heavily made-up this morning, and he noticed her strong hands and well-built figure.

'Have you been to the Greek amphitheatre?' she asked in good English. 'I believe it dates back to the third century BC but later was completely remodelled by the Romans.'

Their conversation was continuing desultorily when Jonathan asked, 'Have you stayed here before?'

'In Taormina? Yes, but not in this hotel.'

Out of the corner of his eye, Jonathan saw Miss Heathcott coming into the courtyard. It was not long before she was standing beside them.

'I'm so glad you have met my friend, Jonathan,' Miss Heathcott remarked with a bright smile. 'Do you mind if I join you both?'

Promptly sitting down and turning to the lady, Miss Heathcott went on: 'I remember seeing you at the hotel a few years ago. Are you by any chance the wife of Signor Renaldi?'

'Who on earth is Signor Renaldi?' the lady answered peremptorily.

'A gentleman who met with an unfortunate

accident here a few days ago – in fact poor Jonathan found him dead in his room on arrival.'

The lady rose from the table. In a disdainful but controlled voice, she said, 'I don't know who the two of you are, but I am finding this conversation disagreeable.'

Miss Heathcott continued to talk on regardless. 'And now we have the terrible shock of poor Bruno, the hotel manager's death. It seems we have all come here at a very sad time.'

Gathering up a jacket from the back of her chair, the lady glared at the other woman. 'I am afraid all this is really not of interest to me. If you're trying to make any personal insinuations, I can assure you I can account for all my movements before and since my arrival.'

'Yes, whatever she knows, I don't doubt she's covered her own tracks more than effectively,' Miss Heathcott muttered as the lady left them without a further glance.

'What makes you think she was the wife of this man Renaldi?'

'Just a guess really, but I seem to have hit the mark. I was working from the fact that I'd seen them both in the hotel that time I was telling you about.'

After a silence, Jonathan said, 'Well, if she's got an alibi, you're running out of suspects as regards people staying or working in the hotel.'

'Am I?' Miss Heathcott gave him an amused look.

'Anyhow,' said Jonathan heatedly, 'what are the guilty people trying to achieve? Two murders – I say two if we assume Bruno's death was not an accident – and how nearer are they to their political aims, that is – again – assuming that is what it's all about?'

'That's what it's about, I can assure you,' Miss Heathcott answered. 'And what are they nearer? Establishing a defined leadership by sorting out a few people before they make their move for independence.'

'So do you reckon you know the killer?'

'Oh, yes.'

'Who, then?'

'Giovanni.'

'The concierge?'

'Talk in the town has always had it that he's an illegitimate descendant of Count Ciano, Mussolini's foreign minister. You will remember that after Mussolini's fall he was shot by partisans in 1944 after a travesty of a trial. The conspirators, the two murdered men,' Miss Heathcott sighed, 'all seem to have had antecedents who were followers of *Il Duce*. What a pity they had to fall out!'

Jonathan didn't remember Count Ciano being shot; in fact he had never heard of him. 'So it was Giovanni who lured Renaldi back to his room after he'd checked out and then shot him? And interfered with Bruno's car?'

Miss Heathcott didn't answer and Jonathan went on: 'So what are you going to do now?'

'Me? As you know, everything's in the hands of the police. I'm just a little old lady here on holiday.'

Back in Rome, Jonathan read in the paper one day that Bruno's death had been established as an accident. The report went on to state that the murder of the man Jonathan had found in his room was still under investigation. Over the following weeks, he noticed no news item concerning an arrest; in fact he never saw any further reference to the matter. Sicily remains a province of Italy. None of his friends at the British Embassy knew anything of a movement for independence. And yet Miss Heathcott had seemed so certain about her theory. Jonathan was left wondering.

Running Away

Bob Thornton motored over to see his old friend
Cecil Bromhead after he had read that morning's
newspaper. They had been fellow officers in the
Wiltshire Yeomanry in the 1914 war. He needed
someone to talk to.

The Germans had launched their attack in the
West only two weeks before, but they were already
encircling the British Expeditionary Force in the
area of Dunkirk. It was 26 May 1940 – just a little
more than twenty one years since he and
Bromhead had returned home after the last war.
They had joined up on the same day and been
demobilised early in 1919. Major Thornton had
suffered a bad leg injury in the first battle of
Mons and been out of action for some time, but
his friend had ended up attached to another
regiment and come out a colonel.

The famous roses in beds all round the house
were well in bud as he drew up outside Tollard
Hall near Salisbury. The Colonel himself, tall, erect,
grey-haired, opened the front door and led him

into the library, a sprawling room taking up half the front side of the house. Two or three Persian carpets on the wooden floor, and closely-packed shelves lined the walls; Bromhead used the room both as his office and informal reception room.

'Cigarette, old boy?' he said, holding out his case.

They both lit up.

It was only eleven o'clock but the host decided it was time for a drink and pulled a bell for the butler.

'When you rang up I guessed why you wanted to come. It's the news, right?'

'Yes,' answered Thornton. 'Where do we stand if we lose our entire army? It'll take months to put together another fighting force, let alone replace all the lost equipment.'

The arrival of a very young-looking butler cut him short.

'Whiskey all right by you?' asked Bromhead.

'What's happened to Dobson?' Thornton enquired as the man withdrew.

Dobson was Bromhead's batman in the 1914 war and had stayed on with him afterwards as butler and general factotum.

'He went back to the yeomanry a couple of months ago. Heard they were looking for ex-NCOs.

In fact, I've applied to rejoin the regiment myself. Eight months of nothing whatsoever happening and now suddenly all this...'

The Colonel brushed some ash off his tweed jacket.

'Thank God we've got Winston at the helm now. If it were left to Chamberlain and Halifax, I expect they'd be suing for peace.'

'Those two are still in the Cabinet,' said Thornton.

'They may be, but Winston's not going to surrender, nor – I should imagine – would the new Labour Party ministers want to.'

They went on talking about the war and the butler was told to bring more whiskey, and this time to leave the decanter on the table.

'I suppose the French should never have gone to war,' observed Bromhead when they were once more on their own. 'It hasn't stopped their never-ending class conflict. There's been little support for the war among the working class and the Right has been pretty unenthusiastic too.'

'I think the Right always feared the Left more than Hitler,' said Thornton. 'There's been a general apathy from the start and that doesn't exactly help things now!'

'What are your own plans?' Bromhead asked.

'I can't join up again with my bad leg, but I'm busy helping organise the LDV in my area, right down as far as the sea.'

'Yes, I've read about them. Local Defence Volunteers, the "Last Ditch Volunteers"!'

'You may laugh,' said Thornton, 'but as a front-line force, especially along our coasts, they're all we've got.'

'I was only pulling your leg,' said Bromhead, hastily insisting his friend should stay for lunch.

Fresh salmon followed by lamb cutlets belied the current food rationing. 'All from the estate,' the host muttered. Small, wiry bachelor Bob Thornton was duly appreciative.

They were served by the same young man who had brought them their drinks.

'Looks a smart lad,' Thornton remarked later by way of conversation.

'Yes, I hope so,' said the Colonel. 'Look, there's something I haven't told you. My son – your god-son, Richard, has gone missing!'

'Missing? Where?'

'Nobody knows. Run off from the school! It's been three days now.'

'You've been a long time telling me.'

'I know. It was rather a relief to talk about something else for a change.'

'I can't remember – how old is he?'

'Seventeen and in his last year. The school are as worried as I am. His housemaster rang me up again this morning. Evidently his form-master has gone to London – of all places – for a couple of days to see if he can find him. Claims to have one or two ideas as to where he might have

140

gone. I gave it my blessing, of course, but we're just clutching at straws. He could have gone anywhere.

'You were asking me about my new butler,' Bromhead went on after a pause. 'Well, he's Dobson's son. Born and bred here, nineteen years old and already enlisted in the yeomanry. Just waiting to be told when to report. You would have seen him in the past – he and Richard were often playing together. I sent him over to the school when I heard about Richard, unofficially of course, to ferret around the local village, see if he could pick anything up, talk to a few of the boys if he could, on their own wavelength, but he came back with nothing. Funny, he too ended up in London, on some tip he'd been given, he said, but it was a false alarm.'

'Has no one any idea as to why he should have run away?'

'Well, I haven't. And the housemaster says he's no idea. Seemed perfectly happy, according to him.'

'Might he have run away to join the army? A bit of that sort of thing with under-age fellows went on in the last war.'

'Unlikely. You know him – a bit of an intellectual, a dreamer if you like. Never hunted, never wanted to come out shooting. Takes after his dear mother more than me, I'm afraid.'

Cecil Bromhead had made a rare mention, Thornton noted, of the wife to whom he had been so devoted and who had died from cancer five years before. Richard had been their only child.

Mr Nelson, Richard's form-master, was forty five years old. He had served in the last war and on demobilisation, at his recently remarried mother's request, had changed his name to that of her second husband. He was the only child of either party and it was all to do with inheritance, she said. Through the good offices of his stepfather, he obtained a place at Cambridge University. A first in Classics gained him his first job as assistant-master at a boys' preparatory school in Surrey. In 1929 he had seen a discreet advertisement in *The Times* by an agency acting for the public school where he now taught. On the strength of his quiet personality and good degree, he was taken on as a form-master in the lower school. Subsequently he was promoted to form-master of the fifth form. He enjoyed teaching the older, more intelligent boys and only gave way in his classroom to other masters for maths and geography lessons. Nelson was tall, thin, with an unruly mop of dark hair. He wore strong glasses and his poor eyesight precluded him from being called upon to take charge of any games. In fact, his only role outside the classroom was acting as second officer in the school Officer Cadet Training Unit. Once a week he put on his old army uniform and drilled the cadets on the parade ground, followed by rifle instruction and battle-field lectures.

He tried not to have favourites among his pupils, but, since the previous term, had formed a certain rapport with Richard Bromhead. Richard was a polite, serious boy and they shared an interest in contemporary English literature. Nelson was unmarried and had not made friends with other masters, so was often lonely. He had started to look forward to the meetings with Richard out-side the classroom. In particular, they both admired the novels and poems of a coterie of writers known as the Bloomsbury set. The fact that Richard had often said how much he would like to meet these authors had set Nelson thinking.

It was a wild notion, but could Richard have gone to London with the idea of trying to see one of them? Anyway, although Mr Nelson knew London far from well – he always spent the school holidays with his widowed mother at her house in Eastbourne – he went up on the train to Waterloo and started his search by calling at every YMCA hostel he could find within reasonable walking distance of the station.

No superintendent had seen or heard of anyone of Richard's name. Might he have registered under a false name? Not possible, he was told. All young men had to show their identity cards. He had more luck with the publisher of the writings of some of the Bloomsbury group, who kindly agreed to find out whether any of his authors knew anything about the boy.

'I sometimes get letters for them here, which I forward on. It's conceivable, I suppose, that if he had written to one or other of them he might have received a reply, from which he could have obtained their address.'

He had been a schoolmaster himself in his younger days and was not unsympathetic. It was agreed Mr Nelson should call back the following day.

In fact, there had been no particular reason that had prompted Richard's running away. He was bored and suddenly had an urge to be free – an overwhelming urge to shake off school routine and disciplines. He was even getting a bit tired of Mr Nelson, but it was awkward refusing to go round to his rooms now and then for a cup of tea. He had decided to leave the school one particular afternoon, and walked to the local station, boarding a train for London. He would go back after a day or two, when his money ran out.

He hadn't given much thought about where he was going to stay. But, on arrival at Waterloo, he certainly knew he was hungry and he queued up to buy a sandwich at a food stall. He was eating it and wandering towards the exit, when he almost literally ran into a young girl coming in the opposite direction.

'Richard!' she shrieked, 'what on earth are you doing here? Isn't it term time?'

Her name was Rachel; she was two years older and the daughter of friends of his father in the country. Last Christmas she had become the first girl he had kissed.

'I'm giving myself a little break. If you want to know, I've run away.'

'You're joking. Does your father know?'

'Don't suppose anybody does at the moment. I won't be missed till roll-call tonight.'

'Are you going to join the army?'

'They haven't quite got down to the seventeen-year-olds yet!'

'Well, I'm about to become a Land Girl,' Rachel announced.

'What the devil's that?'

'Helping full-time on a farm somewhere – wherever I'm sent.'

They went off to find a place where they could sit down and have a cup of tea. Rachel said she could catch a later train home.

Bob Thornton went over to see Cecil Bromhead again three days after his earlier visit, this time a much relieved man. Although there was very little information about it in the papers, from all he had heard about the private boats being pressed into service along the coast, it was evident that an evacuation of the troops from France was under way.

Thornton was visiting at Bromhead's own request. The Colonel was not a keen driver and over the years they had got into the habit of seeing each other at Bromhead's house. 'May be the last you'll see of me for a bit,' he had said over the telephone. It sounded as if he was on the verge of returning to the old regiment. From that call, Thornton had gathered there was still no news of Richard.

The boy's disappearance was indeed the first subject his friend brought up when Thornton was once more comfortably seated in the library at Tollard Hall. This time there was no butler in evidence.

'Have you seen this?' said Bromhead, thrusting a newspaper, folded back at an inside page, into his hands.

Thornton read the headline: 'PUBLIC SCHOOLBOY STILL MISSING AS POLICE SEEK LOCAL GIRL'.

The item was in a small corner of an inner page of that day's *Daily Mail*. The 'story' took up no more than a few lines and gave Richard's name and reported he had been missing from school for five days. It then went on to say that Annie Besant, a young girl working in the village sweet shop near the school, had also disappeared. Her parents were distraught and had called in the police.

146

Thornton had not seen any news item about Richard in his own paper on that day or on any previous days. He was surprised the *Mail* had found room for it, as, like all national newspapers, they were restricted to just a few pages a day, and most papers were printing very little other than war news and speculation about invasion.

'No reason to suppose the two events are connected,' Thornton said at last.

'That's what I told the Chief Inspector when he came to see me yesterday,' replied Bromhead forcefully. 'In fact, knowing Richard, I should think it highly unlikely.'

'Because he's too much of the shy type?'

'Partly that, and also because I don't think he's got to the stage of being interested in girls yet.'

It crossed Thornton's mind that there was always a first time, but basically he had to agree with his friend's judgement.

'I only wish he would get in touch,' the Colonel said morosely. 'I can't think what's got into him. It'll be interesting to see if the famous Mr Nelson – that's his form-master – comes up with anything. I knew nothing of this implied link, of course, when I rang you yesterday to come over. First I knew of it was when the Inspector came round in the afternoon. And now there's this damned publicity...'

Thornton shook his head in commiseration, then changed the subject: 'You said yesterday I might not be seeing you again for a bit.'

147

'Yes, I've been officially recalled. It was pretty sudden, but I'd sorted out all my gear and am reporting to the camp tomorrow. Luckily the tailor in London had my new uniform ready in time. Couldn't get into my old one!'

'Will you still go ahead as planned?'

'Yes, I've got to. But Dobson's coming back this evening. He can stand by the telephone and will let me know if Richard – or anybody else – rings. I've managed to get him a week's leave. You remember how my father turned this place into a convalescent home for officers in the last war? I've offered to do the same now. The Red Cross has accepted and Dobson will be in charge of putting everything into store and getting the house ready for them.'

'Very commendable idea,' said Thornton, lighting a cigarette. 'By the way, you told me how you'd sent Dobson's son over to the school to see if he could find anything out. I wonder if the girl had gone missing then or whether there was any gossip about her and Richard?'

'I've told Dobson to ask him, so I'll know tonight. The boy didn't say anything about it to me, but he's no longer here. He got his order to report the day after you saw him. It's just me and the cook here now. She's staying on with the Red Cross.'

'What with you and young Dobson, the Wiltshire Yeomanry certainly seem to be springing into action!'

'Making up for lost time, I suppose,' Bromhead laughed.

Richard and Rachel were comfortably ensconced in Rachel's parents' flat in London. She had been staying there on her own when she'd met Richard. She knew her parents would not be coming up to town, and realising he had nowhere to go, she changed her plans and invited him to come back with her for the night. Experiencing a surge of reinterest in the small, dark-haired girl, whom he had not seen since Christmas, Richard did not need much persuading.

'Just for tonight!' she had said. 'Tomorrow you must sort yourself out ... go back to school.'

However, they allowed the days to drift by. Richard was falling in love and Rachel was not averse to having a few days of fun before reporting to the Land Army. Then, in the afternoon of the same day that Richard's father was showing the news item about Richard to Bob Thornton, Rachel had bought a *Daily Mail*. Idly looking through the inner pages, she had suddenly seen the headline. 'Oh God!' she said. 'You're in the papers.'

Richard snatched it away to have a look at it.

'Who's this girl?' he said.

'Are you saying you don't know her?'

'If it's who I think it is, she's a little fat blonde, who sometimes serves in the tuck shop. But you can see she hasn't run off with *me*!'

149

'Well, let's hope your father hasn't seen it. Coming on top of everything else...'

Richard said he felt too frightened to speak to his father on the telephone.

'All right, we must go down and see him first thing tomorrow,' said Rachel, swiftly taking command. 'He will know what to do. We've been very selfish and irresponsible. You haven't even told your father where you are.'

Later on, she melted sufficiently to agree to go out to the cinema. They saw Bing Crosby and Bob Hope in *The Road to Singapore* at the Plaza in Lower Regent Street. Afterwards Rachel surprisingly suggested, at her expense – as Richard had exhausted all his money – a farewell dinner at a Soho restaurant. A small band was playing the hit song of the moment, 'I'll Never Smile Again'. Richard hoped it wasn't about to become too appropriate.

He was not looking forward to the confrontation with his father. In the train to Salisbury, he reflected again how wrong he had been in letting a little jaunt away from school develop into what was now a disappearance of six whole days. It was not as if the two of them were even having an affair. He was completely inexperienced and Rachel was a virgin and intended to stay that way. Knowing little about contraception, like him, her great fear was she might have a baby. So the relationship did not go beyond a certain amount of kissing and cuddling. The time had gone so quickly. He was with a lovely girl, free from home ties, free from the oppression of school, just enjoying himself: getting up late, listening to dance music on the wireless, going to cheap restaurants, to the films, having fun doing shopping with Rachel on the one ration book.

The kiss at Christmas time had meant as much to Rachel as it had to him. He had not realised that it was a first kiss for her too. He smiled as he looked back to that wonderful Christmas. Admittedly it had been the coldest anyone could remember, on top of a coal shortage, but his father and Rachel's parents had been all right with log fires burning all day. Then Christmas lunch itself, his father and he as guests at Rachel's parents' house: a succulent turkey, plum pudding with brandy butter, stilton cheese ... crackers, no different from peacetime. Rachel's father had not been slow in keeping his glass filled with a vintage Margaux either, despite his father's occasional frown. And afterwards the walk with Rachel in the garden and, his courage fuelled, that long kiss...

When the young couple arrived at Tollard Hall, Richard's father had already departed for the army. The first person they saw was Major

Thornton, who had decided to come over in case Dobson needed help.

He looked astonished. 'Well, Richard, at least you're alive and in one piece,' he said at length. 'But how come you're here too, Rachel?'

Neither of them replied. Richard was speechless at the sight of two enormous removal vans, with workmen carrying out heavy pieces of furniture. Through the ground-floor windows he could see other men wrapping up items into packing cases.

Dobson came up to them. 'Nice to see you again, Master Richard,' he said with a broad smile.

Major Thornton told Richard his father had left an hour earlier for the yeomanry camp and went on to say the house was being shut down for the duration of the war. 'Within a few days, it will be a convalescent home,' he added.

Dobson broke in to say that a small wing was being retained, with living-room and two bed-rooms, one for the Colonel and one for Richard. His belongings would be carefully moved. This news slightly eased Richard's sense of shock.

Thornton now took hold of Richard's arm and led him inside to the kitchen, with Rachel following. The cook was nowhere to be seen and Thornton told the girl to put the kettle on and make them a cup of tea.

'Now, explain to me what you've been up to,' he said sternly. 'I must get on to your father and tell him you've come back.'

Richard began by saying how school had

suddenly become too much for him and all he had wanted was to get away for a few days, but Thornton quickly interrupted him.

'That doesn't explain why you've waited six days to get in touch with anybody. Your father's been worried to death. And what about this shop-girl – has she been with you?'

'I know nothing about her, I swear,' said Richard.

'The police have been to see your father. There's quite a hunt on for her. And for you too, for that matter.'

Rachel intervened. 'I ran into him quite by chance in London. He's been with me the whole time – at my parents' flat.'

'Do your parents know about this?'

'No. I just told them I was staying on in London for a few days.'

'Well, I hope the two of you have been behaving yourselves,' Bob Thornton grunted, slightly taken aback at the news. 'You, Richard, stay here at the house until I speak to your father. We'll let him ring up your housemaster. As for the police, I think that's best left to your father too.' Then, turning to Rachel: 'As for you, you'd better get on home. Did you let your taxi go?'

'Yes.'

'In that case, I'll drop you off when I go home myself in a little while.'

*   *   *

Mr Nelson, on the day he started out on his trip to London from the school, had been surprised when the girl from the tuck shop joined him in his carriage. He knew who she was and she recognised him as one of the masters, even knew his name.

'What brings you to London?' he asked politely.

'Not that bloke what's run away.' So the news had already spread to the village, Nelson thought. 'No, another young bloke what was down at the shop yesterday looking for him.'

'Someone to do with the school?' Nelson asked.

'Nah. More like he knew him from the holidays, I should say.'

There was a silence, then the girl erupted: 'He's asked me to meet him in London – for a night out like.'

'Do you have to be back by this evening?' asked an intrigued Mr Nelson.

'That'll depend, won't it?' the girl replied archly.

Mr Nelson hid himself behind his paper. Who was this young man, he wondered?

After a while, the girl said, 'Are you staying in London yourself?'

'Yes,' he replied, still holding up his paper and hoping to avert further questions. However, by the time the train reached London, she had managed to get him to tell her the name of his hotel and whereabouts it was.

Early that evening she was knocking on his door. 'The bleeder wasn't where 'e said 'e'd be. I've been waiting three hours.'

'Why are you coming to tell *me* about it?'
'I'm stuck, aren't I? No money to go back home.'
'I suppose I can lend you the fare.'

Fortunately the Colonel in charge of the yeomanry regiment was an old friend of Bromhead's and when Bromhead went to see him and asked for a day's leave of absence on the day after he had arrived, explaining the particular reason, the Colonel agreed readily. He had only been in the camp a few hours when Bob Thornton had succeeded in reaching him on the telephone with the news of Richard's appearance. He had told Thornton to tell his son that, all being well, he would be over in the morning.

Thornton had duly gone off with Rachel, and Richard had set about sorting his belongings in his new room. The removal men had already been instructed by Dobson to move his bed and his various items of furniture. The room had not been used for many years and the cook was at the same time vacuum-cleaning the curtains and the faded carpet. Afterwards he took himself for a long walk over the estate, and by the time he came back the two removal vans were no longer there. He sat down with a book in the library. Apart from his father's desk, this room was being left very much as it was, presumably as a quiet haven for the wounded officers.

The cook prepared him an excellent dinner,

155

which he would have been quite happy to have had in the kitchen, but which Dobson insisted on serving in the dining-room. Soon after, he was in his bed. Forcing himself not to think about the morrow, he slept soundly until Dobson woke him with a cup of tea at eight o'clock.

He was downstairs by nine, to find the removal men back again. They had unloaded and put into their warehouse everything they had collected the previous day, one of them told him, but there was still another full day's work ahead. He was standing outside, watching all the activity, when a taxi drew up. Here's where the trouble starts, he thought; this would be his father.

But it was Mr Nelson from school! What on earth was he doing here? Had the headmaster sent him?

He walked over. The driver paid, Mr Nelson turned round, equally astounded to see his pupil.

'Why have you come here, sir?' cried Richard.

'To tell your father I couldn't find you!' said Nelson.

He went on to explain how he'd been in London looking for him and had decided to call in and see his father before returning to the school. 'Just in case he had any new lead,' he went on. 'I tried ringing up all yesterday, but I was told your father wasn't available and they wouldn't tell me how I could get hold of him. Kept asking me to leave a message.'

Typical Dobson, Richard thought. Hadn't heard of the caller and overdoing the discretion.

'But why did you go to London in the first place?'

'I thought you might have been in touch with one of the Bloomsbury people and I could find you that way. But in the end the publisher told me none of them knew anything about you.'

Richard was nonplussed. 'Come into the house and I'll get you a coffee,' he said in the end.

When Colonel Bromhead arrived half an hour later he found the two of them sitting in the kitchen.

They both rose.

Richard clasped his father, then said, 'Can I introduce my form-master, Mr Nelson?'

'Yes, I've heard of you, but we've never met,' said the Colonel, holding out his hand. 'You went looking for Richard in London, I gather. But I was told yesterday he'd returned of his own accord. How come you're here too?'

'You look very smart in your new uniform, Father,' Richard said out of the blue.

'You've got a lot of explaining to do,' was his father's stern reply, as Mr Nelson started to recite the reason behind his abortive mission.

Dobson entered to announce the arrival of a Chief Inspector. It was the one who had been to see Bromhead a few days before.

'I told him to meet me here when I heard you were back,' Bromhead said to Richard, 'to let him ask all his questions direct and get him out of the way, or hopefully so.'

Dobson was still hovering. 'Ask him to wait a few minutes,' said Bromhead. Then, looking hard at Nelson: 'I've been puzzling where I've seen you before and it's just come to me. It wasn't at the school – it was at Ypres in August 1917, the day before the start of the big battle. But your name was Briggs then, Lieutenant Briggs. You had been posted to our battalion and you were up before me as the senior officer there at the time. A local Frenchwoman back at the base had complained about an assault on her sixteen-year-old daughter and had identified you as...'

'I don't know what you're talking about, sir,' interrupted Nelson vehemently. 'I agree I was on that part of the front – for my sins – but serving under my own name. I've certainly never called myself Briggs. I fear it's a case of mistaken identity.'

' "For my sins" – I seem to remember you used that expression in the mess sometimes,' said Bromhead reflectively. 'I never thought I'd see you again.

'We were short of officers at the time, and I decided to hear the case after the battle which we all knew was about to start. But none of us ever saw you again. We assumed you had been killed and your body not found.'

'This is preposterous,' said Nelson. 'You have found your son, I can do no more, and I will take my leave.'

158

'Hold on a minute,' replied Bromhead. 'Let's see what the Inspector has to tell us.'

The man was shown into the kitchen.

'Well, you can see my son's back, Chief Inspector, so there's no more investigation required on that score. This is his master, Mr Nelson. Now, what news of the missing girl from the village?'

'Still missing, I'm afraid.' The Inspector turned to Richard: 'Your father gave me to understand on the telephone that you know nothing about her disappearance, that at no time was she with you on your journey to London nor whilst you were there. Is that correct?'

'Yes, I swear that is correct.'

'And that in addition you can prove you were with someone else during your entire stay in London?'

'Yes, sir.'

'Mr Nelson's been in London,' remarked Bromhead.

'Were you acquainted with the missing girl?' the Inspector asked.

'No.'

'But surely as a master at the school you would sometimes have seen her in the shop or even spoken to her?'

'I have no recollection.'

'But, sir,' broke in Richard, looking at Mr Nelson, 'we've sometimes been in the shop together and you would have noticed her.'

159

'I suppose I may have done,' said Mr Nelson, making to go. As a last shaft, he said to the Inspector, 'Why are you so sure she went to London anyhow?'

Only that morning the Chief Inspector's superior had again been critical of his lack of success in finding any clues to the mystery, and he was intent on doing something positive.

'I think you had better come along to the station and make a statement,' he said to Nelson.

By lunchtime the Colonel's attitude to his son had thawed a little.

'As you seem so fed up with school, I suggest you don't go back. Would be a bit awkward with Nelson in any case, after what I said to him.'

'Father, if Nelson really *were* Briggs, why did he risk coming here to see you?'

'Heaven knows. He probably didn't connect me with the Major who questioned him. Look, you were due to leave at the end of next term in any event. You could do some war work instead. We'll have to think what.'

'Father, I've already thought. I've become terribly fond of Rachel. She's about to join the Land Army. Wherever she's posted, I'm sure the farmer could do with another pair of hands come next month with all the crops to be cut and brought in. Wouldn't that be all right?'

'What's wrong with helping around here?'

'And after that,' exclaimed Richard, ignoring his father's suggestion, 'I'll be nearly eighteen and I want to join the Air Force!'

'I haven't heard you come up with *that* idea before,' said his father, looking at him curiously.

'Well, I've changed a bit in the last few days, grown up if you like. I want to take my place in life.'

Dobson's son admitted to his father he had spoken to the missing girl in the tuckshop and that he had gone to London during his visit to the school, like he had told the Colonel, but denied he had arranged any rendezvous with her. At the police station the Inspector was getting nowhere with Mr Nelson; and the sombre background to this little story continued to deepen. Although the greater part of the British Expeditionary Force was saved and the troops welcomed home from Dunkirk as heroes, they had left behind almost all their weapons. In addition, both the Royal Navy and the RAF had suffered grievous losses. The French were not expected to hold out much longer.

Reviewing the situation in Parliament, Mr Churchill warned of an imminent threat of invasion. But Napoleon had failed, and so too would Hitler, he said.

*   *   *

The weeks went by. On 22 June France signed an armistice. By then, Richard was working, as he had planned, on a large arable farm in Wiltshire alongside Rachel. Colonel Bromhead never disclosed to the Inspector his suspicions of Mr Nelson's involvement in the village girl's disappearance. It was all too fanciful, he decided. She never returned to where she had come from and the mystery was only solved some three months later after one of the early bombing raids on London. Her body was found by ARP workers clearing the ruins of a line of houses in South London. Neighbours were able to identify her and the police picked up her name from the lists of victims supplied to them routinely by the Home Office. The case was closed. Mr Nelson learnt about her death when he was in the shop one day buying cigarettes and overheard two customers talking. Indeed, she *had* spent that night with him in his hotel room, but at her urging just as much as his, he felt. Anyway, she had departed cheerfully enough the next morning, borrowing some money off him and saying she was intending to stay on in London. She did not elaborate on her plans and he did not enquire what they were.

After he joined the RAF later in 1940, Richard lost touch with Rachel. He heard she had become engaged to a young farmer. His strange, short life was ended in December 1941 over Benghazi in the Western Desert, when he was shot down attempting to draw fire from a German fighter attacking a badly damaged plane in his own squadron. He was awarded a posthumous DFC. Colonel Bromhead survived the war and by the time it was over had been promoted to Brigadier. He was proud of his son and, with the passage of time, lost any resentment he felt over the schoolboy escapade. In fact, he came to admire Richard's initiative in stealing what were to become, quite probably, his happiest days.

St Valentine's Day

St Valentine's Day commemorates the day on which the Roman priest, Valentine, was beheaded in AD 270. It is remembered each year on 14 February. According to legend, birds mate on that day. Sweethearts are chosen on that day too. With a recipient sometimes not even aware of another's feelings, traditionally an unsigned letter would come, expressing love and devotion.

Toby, a bachelor of some thirty years, was living in the twenty-first century, so it was not a letter he received, but a rather garish card decorated in green and pink and depicting two young people gazing wistfully into each other's eyes. He had been going through his morning mail in the usual way and had been startled when he slit open an envelope and found this card, with 'Happy Valentine's Day' written inside, but, in the old-fashioned way, unsigned. His first thought was, Who on earth could have sent it to him? The neatly typed envelope gave no clue. In his mind he went through old girlfriends, then nephews

165

and nieces, male friends, anyone he could think of who might be playing a joke. He was on the point of laughing the whole thing off, when he heard a key turn in his front door.

It was the woman who came twice a week at this time of morning to clean his flat, do some ironing and generally tidy up all the mess he had left since her previous visit.

'You'll never guess,' he said, by way of making conversation, 'I've been sent a Valentine's card!'

'Do you know who it's from?' the lady responded.

For some reason he started to think of her daughter, a married woman in her mid-forties, who had once come to clean for him when her mother was ill.

'No idea,' he said, 'I'll probably never know.'

Toby was a writer and kept no particular hours. At around nine o'clock every morning he was in the habit of wandering out to a coffee shop, run by some Italians. The next day he was sitting down having his usual *café latte* and one croissant, when he noticed the cleaning woman's daughter walk in. He had never seen her there before. Strange that he had been thinking about her the previous day.

'Come and sit down with me,' he called out. After an initial puzzled look, she bought whatever she wanted and promptly did so. He made some small talk and then said suddenly, 'Yesterday was Valentine's Day. I got a card!'

The woman looked blank. 'You're lucky,' she said. 'It's been a long time since I got one. In fact,' she went on after a silence, 'I only wish there was someone out there who'd like to send me one. My life's in a pretty good mess at the moment.'

He remembered her name was Mandy. She was not unattractive. Her figure was starting to run to fat, and wrinkles had formed under her eyes, but she exuded an air of well-being. He knew from her mother, who was fond of talking about her, that she had a daughter aged fourteen called Kathy.

'So is your daughter giving you trouble?' Toby asked.

'She gives no more trouble than any girl of that age.'

That left the husband. 'What's your husband do?' Toby probed.

'He's a long-distance lorry driver. Meant to earn a lot of money, but I don't seem to see very much of it. He's on the Continent a lot, turns up at all hours of the day and night, always expecting me to be there ready for him. Life seems one mass of fights.'

'What are you doing this morning?'

'Very little, as usual. Nothing to do really, bar some shopping, till Kathy comes home from school at three and I get her her tea.'

'When will you next see your husband?'

'Oh, I dunno. In a few days perhaps. He's in

Germany at the moment. Sometimes I feel I'd just like to get away from everything. Park my daughter with some friends and get out into the world and live a little.

'I'm afraid you've caught me on a bad morning,' she concluded with a wry smile.

Toby had recently finished his latest book and delivered it to his agent. Presumably it had now got as far as his publishers, although as yet he had heard no word either from them or the agent. He had deliberately made the type of plot, even the style, very different from his earlier novels. It was his first effort to break away from the mundane, to make his work more – for want of a better word – literary. How it would be received by the publishing firm, he did not know. But he knew that he was proud enough of it. Perhaps seeking some sort of reassurance, on the spur of the moment he invited Mandy to come to his house. 'I'll read you the opening pages of my new novel and you can tell me whether you like it,' he said. 'Feel free to give me any criticisms.' It was people like Mandy who had been buying his earlier books, so what harm in trying the new one out on her?

Nodding and without making any comment, she gathered up her things and they made their way back.

'It all seems very much as I remember it,' she

said, going into the kitchen. 'Let's have another cup of coffee.'

Mandy had become relaxed and quite at home as they settled into two armchairs and he started to read aloud. The ring of the telephone startled them both. It was Esmerelda, an erstwhile girl-friend whom he had not seen for many months, who announced she was coming round right away. Toby started to protest – it was not possible, he was in the middle of working – but then suddenly thought it would be amusing for his old flame to see Mandy, to realise that his life with the opposite sex hadn't come to a complete halt with their breakup. 'Yes, come by all means,' he ended up saying, 'I'm intrigued to know what's so important that you've got to see me suddenly like this.'

That led him into telling Mandy about the other girl. They'd been together for about two years, he said, but there had been too many rows, often over next to nothing; her fiery temperament had been too much for him. (That at any rate was how Toby liked to think of it; in fact, Esmerelda had walked out on *him.*)

'Funny, my Mum never mentioned her to me,' remarked Mandy.

'She wouldn't have seen her. She never lived here as such.'

'Do you want me to go?'

'Certainly not.'

He went on reading to her. Mandy appeared absorbed and made no interruptions. After a quarter of an hour, the doorbell rang and he let in a grinning, excited Esmerelda. 'I'm engaged,' she shouted, 'and I wanted you to be the first to know!' Toby led her into the sitting-room. She was a bit taken aback when she saw Mandy sitting there.

Toby introduced them and explained that Mandy was helping him with opinions on his new book. He made Esmerelda a cup of coffee in the kitchen and heard her remarking on his Valentine's card, which was standing up on a piece of furniture. Then they both had to hear about this wonderful man in Esmerelda's life. However, she was obviously put out at not finding Toby alone and it was not long before she made her departure.

'Who's your new girlfriend?' she said as they reached the front door. 'Didn't take you long to find somebody else.'

'I could say the same to you,' Toby laughed.

Mandy was equally intrigued about the tall, red-headed, self-assured Esmerelda. 'I wonder you let her go,' she said. He realised she was probably now looking at him with new eyes. He was pleased when she suddenly remarked how she was enjoying listening to his book.

Happy and relieved with the reaction of this one unsophisticated member of the public, he suddenly turned to her and said, 'Next time your husband is off on his travels, why don't we go away together for a few days?' The words were hardly out of his mouth when he regretted having said them. Looking at her, he was not particularly enamoured. Was it because he had been stuck at his desk for so long, rarely seeing anyone, writing, but also worrying about how the publisher would regard his new style? Yes, all that; but he also needed a girlfriend.

Mandy was in no way disconcerted. 'Where had you in mind?' she smiled.

'I don't know – Paris, Rome, New York, where would you like to go?'

Mandy had never been to any of these places, but they settled on Paris. It was somewhere she had always wanted to go and also, as she might have to watch her time away, it was somewhere that did not take too long to get back from.

'Well, it's a question of when,' said Toby. 'In my job, my time's my own, but you'll have to let me know when it's suitable for *you*. Look, I go to that coffee shop every morning. Why don't you drop in when you know a date and I can fix everything up? I'm already looking forward to it,' he put in as an afterthought.

'I think I am too,' said Mandy. 'And now – I'm afraid it doesn't sound very romantic – I must go to the supermarket and get on with my shopping.'

'Er ... probably best to say nothing to your mother,' Toby murmured.

171

Mandy made no reply, but stood up and gave him a kiss on the cheek.

All of the next week he was looking out for her, but no Mandy. *Fool, why hadn't he given her his telephone number?* But that wouldn't have guaranteed she would have rung him up, he supposed. He had suddenly become excited at the idea of the trip and the prospect of seeing Mandy again. Was she ill? Had she had an accident? He had to force himself not to ask the mother any questions. Perhaps she had just changed her mind.

Some Saturdays Toby did not work, did not get up early, but that Saturday he was sitting down as usual in the café. It was nothing like so crowded as usual. After a bit he saw Mandy walk in with a rather squat, untidy-looking man. Her husband? The man said a few words to her and went out again. Mandy placed her order, looked round and came and sat down beside him.

'I'm so sorry it's taken me so long,' she said, 'He had a week off and it's been terribly difficult to get away.'

They agreed to go away for a few days in the middle of the following week. Toby already knew by heart the times of the morning planes, and they chose an early one. 'Give me your mobile number and I'll ring you to confirm I've booked the seats. When would be a good time? I presume you've got a passport!' he added. She nodded and

172

he spelt out exactly where he would be waiting for her.

'I haven't got any particularly smart clothes,' Mandy said, with a worried look.

'Don't worry, it will be a pleasure for me to buy you some.'

'I'll have to hide them when I get back home!' she giggled.

It was eventually agreed she would ring *him*. Toby had obtained the desired tickets on the Internet and printed them out. He then rang up a three star hotel he knew in the rue Chauteaubriand, at the top of the Champs Elysées, and was able to book a suite. When the morning came, he was duly waiting at Terminal 1 by the BA information desk. It was not long before Mandy appeared, carrying a small case. 'I allowed far too long to get here by the Underground – I've just been having a coffee,' she said.

They held hands in the plane. He took a taxi at the airport. They had their first kiss in the sitting-room of their suite, after the porter had brought up the luggage. The suite was spacious enough and had been recently refurbished. After they had unpacked and had a wash, Toby said, 'Let's go out and see the town!'

They walked down to the Rond Point and stopped for a light lunch in a café-bar. They saw something Mandy liked in the window of a shop, but ended up buying something completely different – an expensive short evening dress, which Toby paid for on his credit card, wondering at the same time whether she would ever wear it back home. With his encouragement, she made several other purchases in various shops before they eventually returned to the hotel. Actual sightseeing, he realised, had not been much to the fore.

She wore the dress that night and looked magnificent in it. It was a mild evening and they walked out to have dinner at Fouquet's, a restaurant not far from their hotel. Afterwards he said he knew of a night-club they could go to, but Mandy said she was tired and had had enough for one day. In fact, when he came out of the bathroom and approached their bed, she was sound asleep. He got in beside her, hoping she might wake up, but she went on sleeping peacefully. After a while, he dropped off himself.

She was awake before him. He woke to see her half sitting up and looking at him fondly. 'Well, when are you going to make love to me?' she said.

They had breakfast served in their room and when they were dressed took a bus to the foot of the hill of Montmartre. They climbed the innumerable steps to reach the village. In the small main square they watched the painters busy on their canvases. Surprisingly few had any talent, Toby thought. They went inside the Sacré Coeur and then down to the broad terrace with its sweeping view over the whole of Paris. Mandy seemed ecstatically happy.

Toby noticed a taxi parked nearby and asked the driver if he could take them to Versailles, wait for them and then bring them back to central Paris. The man seemed only too agreeable. Toby would pay meter charges only; payment for waiting would be at Toby's discretion. They toured the palace and wandered round the impressive formal gardens; then went to lunch in a restaurant. Their driver was waiting at the agreed spot and put down his paper, smiling, and got out to open the back seat door for them.

The next day they took the plane back to England. They both felt a little worse for wear after a late night drinking and dancing at a fashionable disco. Mandy assured Toby that her husband would still be away and they went direct from the airport to her flat. She told him to make himself at home and he sat down thinking about the difficulties of continuing the relationship; that was assuming he wanted it to continue. After a while, she was still in the kitchen and he called out, asking if he could go to the bathroom. She shouted out cheerful directions.

The bathroom was not difficult to find in the small flat. As he came out, he saw a half-open bedroom door and looked inside. From the posters on the wall, the small PC and the general mess, it was evidently the daughter's. Looking round the walls, he saw to his horror several pictures of himself, stuck up along with posters of one or two recognisable film stars and, he presumed, members of pop groups.

As he turned, Mandy was behind him.

'I didn't want you to see that,' she said.

'Where did she get those photos of me?'

'She'd heard a lot about you from her grandma, who incidentally is quite a fan of yours, and saw you twice being interviewed on TV. Then she read an article about you in the *Daily Mirror* when your last book was published – two of the photos came from that.'

'Just as well I'm not meeting her,' Toby said awkwardly.

'Oh, I dunno – she'd love it. Here, I'll show you a picture of her.'

Mandy did some rummaging in a drawer and brought out a coloured photograph. Toby knew the daughter was fourteen, but the face and figure in front of him were those of a young girl several years older. Made-up, short blonde hair, a cheeky smile, with a cleavage showing over-developed breasts.

'And still a schoolgirl...' he murmured.

'Yes, I'll be going to collect her later from where she's staying.'

Earlier he had let the taxi go and Mandy now insisted on giving him a cup of coffee in the sitting-room. His Valentine's card! Had he suddenly solved the mystery?

'I wonder if it was by any chance your daughter who sent me that Valentine's Day card?' he said.

'Good Lord, no. That was me!'

Toby was stunned as she went on: 'I had only seen you the once, that time I came to clean for you, but my Mum was talking about you the whole time and I guess I got a bit of a crush on you like my daughter. I knew the address and for a laugh I sent you a card. Then I thought it would be fun to see you again – you might tell me how I could get away from my husband and change my life – so I decided to go to that café of yours. My Mum told me you always went there...'

'Why should I have been able to help you change your life?'

'Well, I suppose being an author and all that.' She paused. 'You might have been able to think of something.'

They said goodbye with vague assurances on Toby's part about keeping in touch. Her talk about changing her life had unsettled him. Of one thing he was sure: he did not want it to involve him. That daughter, for one thing. And, anyway, she wasn't even a single mother; she was *married*!

Going through the post on arrival back at his house, he recognised a letter from his agent. He tore open the envelope. The letter would be about the reaction of his publisher to his new book. He couldn't believe what he read: the publisher, the man who had made so much money from all his earlier efforts, was turning it down!

Within minutes he was on the telephone.

'He didn't say he didn't like it,' the assured middle-aged woman was saying, 'it's just so far away from what your public expects...'

'But what do we do now?' Toby interrupted. 'I can't rewrite the whole thing over again.'

'You're well-known – you've got a name. There are plenty of other publishers. I'll have to start submitting it elsewhere.'

'But they'll all guess the reason why – and that won't help my chances.'

Toby felt so dejected he broke off the conversation and told his agent he'd come back to her; he wanted time to think.

Who could he talk it over with? He rang up Esmerelda. Like him, she was an author. In fact, they had first met at a literary festival, where they were both on the panel of speakers. She agreed to come round.

'Have you got another copy of the typescript?' she asked, after Toby had woefully related his predicament.

He nodded.

'Then let me take it away and read it. Knowing you, it's not going to be *bad* – just different.'

'And then what?'

'Together we'll think of something,' Esmerelda answered brightly.

When Esmerelda departed, it struck him that

he had not been very sympathetic over Mandy's problems that morning, so he wrote her a brief note saying how much he had enjoyed their time together. He even touched on some of their more intimate moments, but he made no mention of the future.

Esmerelda reappeared two days later. 'It's more like the sort of stuff I write,' was her initial comment. 'But it's good! I enjoyed every page of it. In my view, the best thing you've done.'

However, she agreed it might be awkward approaching another publisher. He had become too identified with the firm he was with. 'But I'm in a rush now,' she went on. 'I really came round to ask you if I could hang on to the typescript for a bit and to tell you to cheer up. For the present, why don't you start on a new novel – in your normal format? If nothing else, it'll keep your mind busy.'

'And what about this particular book?'

'Well, from a publisher's point of view, it's short. Your man might be more amenable if you agreed to lengthen it somehow.'

'And ruin it!'

'I wouldn't argue with you.'

'So what shall I do?'

'Leave it to little old Esmerelda. I'll come and see you again in a few days' time.'

Toby gave her a hug as they said goodbye. It

felt good to be sharing his troubles with someone who had once been so close to him. Her visit lifted him out of his depression.

Later, he was rung up by Mandy. 'You've gone very quiet on me,' she said. 'But I appreciated your letter.'

'I came back to find I've run into trouble with my latest book – that one I was reading to you.'

'What sort of trouble?'

'It may be difficult to get it published.'

'Oh, that's a pity.'

'It's more than a pity. It's been a big blow to my self-esteem and, on a more mundane note, it means I'll have no fresh income this year.'

'Oh!'

'Why d'you say "oh" like that?'

'I was hoping you could give me some money.'

'That shouldn't be too difficult. How much?'

'Ten thousand pounds.'

'*Ten thousand pounds?*'

'Well, to start with.'

'What do you mean "to start with"?'

'I've decided to leave my husband and I'll need money to set myself up somewhere else, won't I? You never know what a move like that is going to cost.'

'I'm afraid ten thousand pounds is quite out of the question,' Toby said firmly. 'You've probably been reading in the papers about authors who make vast sums of money, but I'm afraid I'm not one of them. I've got very limited capital behind me.'

There was a silence, then Mandy said, 'I suppose my daughter and I could always come and live with you.'

'That wouldn't be possible, I'm afraid.'

'Why not?'

'It just wouldn't be.'

'Oh well, there's nothing to be done then, is there?'

'I'm afraid not.'

'When am I going to see you again?'

Toby felt the time had come to be firm.

'Look, Mandy, you're a great girl and we had a wonderful time together, but I think it's best to end it all now ... before everything becomes too difficult for us.'

'Goodbye then,' said Mandy after a long pause.

'Goodbye.'

Esmerelda came back to see him, unannounced, the following week. Following her advice, he was attempting a draft of a new book, more on the lines of what his publishers would expect. He was not finding it easy going. He had a new problem on his mind.

'I hope you don't mind, but I gave your typescript to Caroline to read,' she began.

'Caroline? Your literary agent?

'Yes, and, although she's only half-way through, she likes it! She and I are going to have a talk about what to do when she's finished.'

'When will that be?'

'Hopefully in a few days' time.'

Toby was pleased at the news of some positive action, but glumly passed Esmerelda a letter. 'Read this,' he said. 'All I need at the moment.'

Esmerelda unfolded the letter. It was short and written on a computer, signed in ball-point pen 'Mandy':

Dear Toby

I am feeling so disappointed at you not being able to help me. If £10,000 is too much, could you manage £5,000? I was really counting on you. The last thing I want to do is make any trouble.

'Is this that girlfriend I met here once?' asked Esmerelda. 'And what trouble could she make for you?'

Toby related how he had taken her to Paris.

'Surely she cannot blackmail you over that?'

'Blackmail?'

'It sounds like it to me.'

Toby explained he had subsequently written her a letter.

'Was it indiscreet?'

'I suppose so ... rather.'

'Who the hell is this girl? You must have been mad to start writing to her.'

'I didn't think. I felt sorry for her.'

'Well, the trouble she could make for you is to go to some scurrilous newspaper and see if they'd give her some money for it . . . plus her – doubtless highly embellished – account of the whole trip.'

Toby remonstrated that his doings were hardly of interest to the general public.

'Don't you kid yourself,' said Esmerelda severely. 'You're a pretty well-known popular author.'

Toby let Esmerelda go on talking. Eventually he was forced to agree that, whilst the story was not of sufficient interest to fetch one of the vast sums sometimes bandied about, it was nevertheless probably worth £10,000, perhaps even more. Esmerelda summed up by saying the only answer was to try and get his letter back. She wasn't going to let him pay the money and she didn't want to risk seeing his reputation harmed in a newspaper.

At this last remark, Toby couldn't help saying with a smile, 'It's nice to hear you being so solicitous.'

'Why shouldn't I be?' Esmerelda retorted.

'It's not as if we mean very much to each other these days.'

'If you're talking about my engagement – that's off! I couldn't stand the idea of living with that man for the rest of my life!'

Get the letter back, Esmerelda had said. Would

183

Mandy be keeping it in her bag? A possibility, thought Toby, but it would mean seeing her again and then somehow snatching the bag. No, he would have to assume she was hiding it somewhere in her flat. But how to get into the flat?

He went to see a burglar to whom he had been referred (by a local publican), when seeking help on the description of a break-in for one of his earlier novels. Still at the same address and now a respectable night-watchman, or so he claimed, the man recognised him immediately and let him into his small house in Whitechapel. For a modest payment, Toby came away with an instrument, which would allegedly open any straightforward lock, including, more importantly, a Yale or similar front door lock.

The following afternoon, arriving at Mandy's apartment, he was relieved to see the lock was of the Yale variety and that there was no other lock that had to be negotiated. Better ring the bell first though, he decided.

After a while the door was opened by a young girl, whom he recognised as Mandy's daughter.

'Ah, it's Toby,' she said. 'Don't mind if I call you Toby? I've got your picture up on my wall.'

'Lovely to meet you,' said Toby. 'It's Kathy, isn't it? I've heard all about you from your granny.'

'If you want my ma, she's not here,' Kathy remarked. 'Said she wouldn't be back till later.'

'Do you mind if I come in?'

Once inside, she offered him a half-consumed

bottle of a fizzy orange drink. Toby swallowed a mouthful appreciatively.

'I can get you another one if you like.'

'No, this one's fine for the moment. I came here once before,' said Toby, 'and I think I may have left something behind. Can I have a look round?'

'Where would you have left it?'

'I think either in this room or possibly your mother may have taken it into the bedroom. Can I have a quick look in the bedroom?'

The girl's attention had been reclaimed by a noisy videotape playing on the television and she barely answered.

In the bedroom, he quickly searched through the clothes cupboard and all the drawers in various bits of furniture. Back in the sitting-room, he asked innocently, 'Is there anywhere special your mother keeps small items of value?'

'How d'ya mean?'

'Say somewhere where she keeps things locked up?'

'She does that all right. The whole time, trying to stop me eating. There's a cupboard in the kitchen, but I don't know where she puts the key.'

'You carry on watching that film,' Toby said. 'I'll just go and have a look.'

He found a small cupboard high up in the kitchen, which seemed the only one to be locked. Standing on a chair, he got out the implement he had been given and unlocked the door without difficulty. Inside was an untidy mixture of piles of chocolate, packaged sweets and cereals. At the bottom he found his letter, still neatly enclosed in its envelope. He removed some bars of chocolate as well as the letter, wondering whether the tool would be capable of locking as well as unlocking. To his surprise it was.

He was putting the chair back in position when Kathy walked in.

'Here's some chocolate for you,' he said.

'Where'd you find it?'

'In a drawer, but don't tell your mother I gave it to you. In fact, don't tell her I've been here. It's our secret!'

Grabbing the chocolate, the girl said, 'Yes, our secret! Give me a kiss, mister!'

Jumping up, her arms were round his neck and a sticky mouth was being pressed on his. He tried to force her away, but could not avoid a second attack.

She let go an equally sticky hand from his as he made his way out of the front door, asking belatedly if he had found what he had lost. Toby mumbled about it not being important and only just missed another fierce embrace.

Toby telephoned Esmerelda when he was back home. 'I've got the letter!' he shouted. 'What shall I do with it?'

'I want you to show me the ashes in the grate

when I come over ... which will be in ten minutes flat!'

In actual fact, it was nearer half an hour before Esmerelda appeared, with Toby waiting impatiently.

'Sorry, I had to stop off at Caroline's and get your typescript back,' she said. 'Here you are. We don't want to leave it with her until we decide what to do.'

She couldn't stop laughing while Toby was recounting how he had snatched his letter back.

'Can't think how you ever wanted to take up with that girl in the first place,' Esmerelda eventually remarked. 'Perhaps you were missing me.'

'May have been the reason.'

'You don't sound very sure.'

'I could easily say it was the reason, but – to be honest – I don't know. But I know now, looking at you this minute, that I wish we'd never broken up. I'll never find anybody like you again.'

'You might not have to.'

'What?'

'Go looking for somebody else.'

'You mean?' Toby could hardly believe his ears.

'I mean I love you, stupid.'

He pulled her on to the sofa.

'Let's get down to the business of your book,' Esmerelda said after a while, still holding Toby's hand. 'In a nutshell, Caroline is sure she can find a publisher for it. It'll mean you having to leave

187

your agent, as well as your current publishers. Would you mind that? Personally, I feel if you plan to carry on writing in this new way, it can't do any harm making a clean start somewhere else. But you may be in the middle of some contract for a certain number of books, of course.'

'If they refuse to publish one of them, I can break that,' said Toby.

'Caroline said that it read like something I had written,' Esmerelda laughed. 'She said she could get it on the move tomorrow if it had been by me! Perhaps you have subconsciously taken my style,' she added mischievously.

'I'm not going to be drawn by that remark,' smiled Toby. 'You know perfectly well I've never read any of your books ... or not properly.'

Esmerelda grabbed a cushion from the sofa and started hitting him over the head.

He caught hold of her and started kissing her again. When they stopped, Toby said, 'A thought's just come to me. If we are to be – er – married, does it really matter who wrote it? Caroline could get it published under *your* name.'

Esmerelda gave him a look of astonishment.

'I'm about to marry a famous author, soon to become more famous, and respected as well. All I want to do is help him, in his own right, on his new career.'

'Yes, I suppose in a way I *am* trying to start a new career.'

'Of course you are. And with a silly girl who

188

threw you over once and has regretted it ever since.'

'I love you,' said Toby.

'I love you,' Esmerelda repeated.

Death in the Rough

David Handley selected a number four iron club out of his golf-bag as his opponent prepared to drive off on the thirteenth tee. He knew how important it was to keep straight. If the ball ended up more than a few feet off the fairway on either side, it was as likely as not to end up lost. He watched as his friend, Ian Dobbie, using his driver, slammed the ball down the middle. All right, David said to himself, your ball's not going to go so far, but just concentrate on keeping it in play.

On some golf courses 'the rough' means no more than grass slightly longer than on the fairway, scattered with a few spindly trees. On this particular course in North Devon, however, several of the holes were bordered by thick undergrowth, which over the years had been allowed to spread out on to the long grass beside the fairway.

David had deliberately aimed a bit left, but why was it he always managed to drive to the right at this hole? The ball wouldn't even be in the undergrowth but above and beyond it, into the copse behind.

'Probably lost,' remarked Ian Dobbie. 'Play another one.'

Over-cautious, David didn't hit his next ball very far, but at any rate it was on the fairway.

'Now it's your turn to do some work, Trooper,' he said to his black Labrador, as he and Dobbie walked off the tee. He felt a headache coming on and wished he hadn't had that large brandy in the clubhouse before setting out.

It was a warm, sunny Sunday morning in early September and the dog bounded ahead of them. When they reached the approximate spot where David had seen his ball finish its swerve to the right and disappear, he gestured to the dog to go into the bushes, crying out, 'Seek, seek'. Presently the animal started to emit excited howling sounds, but instead of coming out with the ball, as they both hoped, he seemed determined not to move. Thinking the dog might be trapped, David gingerly made his way towards where the noise was coming from. With Dobbie following behind, and David hacking at the tangled brambles with his golf-club, he eventually came into the copse. A few feet away, the dog was wagging his tail and standing over what looked like a dead body.

David was too shocked to move. Dobbie drew alongside him, and then walked forward on his own. David saw him turn the body over and examine it.

White in the face, he walked back to David. 'It's Edward Grayling,' he said. 'Been killed by a blow to the left temple.'

A shaken David grabbed his dog and slipped a length of chain from his pocket into its collar. They heard shouts as they made their way back to the fairway.

It was the two players behind them, calling 'fore!' and asking if they could come through. David and Dobbie waved them on and stood to the side as each one drove off.

When the pair came abreast, Ian Dobbie walked over to them.

'Got some bad news,' he said. 'Just found Edward dead in that wood over there.'

'Edward? Grayling?' spluttered one of the two men. His name was Lord Ancaster and he and his partner were playing their regular Sunday morning round. 'Better go and have a look.'

Ancaster was an elderly, heavily built man, but was soon crashing through the undergrowth. Dobbie followed him. David Handley and Ancaster's partner remained where they were.

'Looks like murder,' announced a dishevelled Ancaster on his return. 'Don't know whether he was killed there or his body taken there. But we'd better go and report it.'

* * *

193

Edward Grayling was captain of the golf club and a retired solicitor. Going bald, and with his rimless spectacles, he looked older than his sixty-odd years. He was also chairman of the committee and most of the members were only too pleased to have him running the club and sorting out any problems. The course was typical of the few in that wild area of Devon: undulating and sloping fairways, but on the whole well maintained, with greens regularly cut and rolled. The land was held by the club on a Crown lease going back to the early part of the twentieth century. There was a small membership of about two hundred people. The interior of the club house consisted of no more than a large stone-floored bar with a collection of tables and chairs, and a dining-room, open for Saturday and Sunday lunches only; on other days sandwiches could be ordered. Although the income helped keep subscriptions down, members enjoyed complaining about holiday-makers coming to play in the summer months.

When the four men got back to the clubhouse, Ancaster told the bar steward to telephone the local constabulary and report a suspected murder. 'But first you can give us all some drinks,' he added. He took himself home when he had finished his glass, and it was agreed that Dobbie would be on hand for the arrival of the police.

After a while, David Handley and Ancaster's partner also left. Then, turning to the steward,

Dobbie enquired, 'How soon do you think they'll be here?'

'It's a Sunday, sir. The man on duty said he was on his own and would come round as soon as he could.'

'Well, I need to go and see someone,' said Dobbie. 'Look, here's the phone number. Ring me when the policeman arrives.'

Still young, very tall, brushing back his black hair with his hand, he walked slowly to the car-park. He settled himself into his sleek new Lexus and turned on the ignition. He made his way to the house of Wing Commander Tommy Byecroft and his wife Daphne.

Daphne opened the door.

'What a wonderful surprise, Ian!' she cried. 'But Tommy's out for the day – playing golf over at Elveston Sands.'

'Just as well,' said Ian. 'I really wanted to talk to you on your own.'

Ian was in love with Daphne. He was sure she felt the same way towards him. On the spur of the moment, and for the first time ever, he drew her towards him and gave her a kiss on the lips. She did not push him away.

'You know there's no future in our behaving like this, darling,' she said eventually. 'I could never leave Tommy and I'm not really one for affairs.'

'Sorry, I got carried away,' Ian said, trying to look sheepish. 'It's Tommy I've come to see you about. Let's sit down somewhere. We found Edward Grayling dead in a wood on the golf course this morning.'

'Good God,' said Daphne, 'was it natural causes?'

'No, looked like murder!'

'But who on earth could have done it?'

'I was wondering about Tommy. The whole club knows how Grayling did everything he could to block Tommy's membership and how Tommy hated him for it.'

'Yes, but Tommy would hardly kill him for that. That's going a bit too far.'

'I just wanted you to be forewarned and to warn Tommy. The police may want to interview him one day if they hear about the animosity. The thing is it would have needed a strong man to have taken Grayling to where he was found, assuming, as I personally do, he was not killed on that spot.'

'When d'you think he was killed?'

'From a brief look at the body, I should say not more than two days ago.'

The telephone rang. 'That'll be for me,' said Ian, hurriedly getting to his feet.

'A police constable is here, sir,' the steward intoned.

'OK, I'll be right back.'

Daphne was looking bewildered over what she had been told. Taking her hand and giving her another kiss, this time on the cheek, Ian explained he had to go back to the club and promised to telephone her once he was home. What a beautiful girl she was, with her perfect figure and long blonde hair. She was in her early thirties, and probably over twenty years younger than her husband.

A uniformed constable was sitting in the bar of the clubhouse, having a cup of tea. There were no other people around. He rose as Ian Dobbie introduced himself.

The steward was standing behind the bar. 'A very sad business, sir,' he remarked.

'It certainly is,' Dobbie replied. 'You've probably known him longer than any of us.'

'Coming up for thirty years I've been here now and never seen anything like it.'

'Well, now, can I take you to where the body is lying?' Dobbie said to the constable.

The constable looked at him sternly. 'I'd like to take a statement from you first, sir, if you don't mind,' he said. Getting out pencil and notebook from an inside pocket, he suggested they should sit down at the table where he was having his tea. When the statement was completed, they set off across the course towards the fairway near which the discovery had been made. They were obliged to stop several times to avoid being hit by balls in play on other fairways.

'He may have to remain where he is until tomorrow,' pronounced the constable, when they came to the body. 'It could be difficult getting hold of anybody senior on a Sunday afternoon. Probably the earliest we can expect is for an Inspector to come over from Exeter in the morning, with whoever he wants to bring. Then he can be moved. I'll report it and see what they say, but it'll probably end up with me coming back tonight and covering the body with a plastic sheet and marking the area with keep out signs.'

'Do you have any idea who might have done it?' he asked Ian as they walked back. Receiving no reply, he added: 'Suppose he might have been hit by a golf ball.' Ian glanced at him with surprise.

Ian's house was only ten minutes away. He rang up Daphne once inside. 'Doubt if we'll know much until tomorrow,' he told her. 'Didn't see any top brass when I got back to the club – just the local bobby.'

'You've got me worrying about Tommy,' she said. 'I'll certainly give him your warning.'

Ian lived on his own. He was thirty-five years of age and had done no work of any kind since inheriting a large sum of money on his mother's death. If pressed, he would claim that golf was his work. He was obsessed with the game. A member of various clubs, he played four or five times a week. Once he had been married, but his wife had left him after two years to go back to the man to whom she had previously been engaged. This was when he was studying to become a doctor. Angry, and despite two years of work completed, he gave it up. He then decided to try and qualify as a barrister and this time patiently saw the whole course through. He passed the exams, but had never practised. Ian had a keen enough brain. However, any will to work was marred by an inherent idleness, cushioned by his inheritance.

He had finished talking to Daphne when the doorbell rang.

It was David Handley. 'Mind if I come in?' he said. 'Just wondered how you got on with the police.'

'Bit of a non-starter really. As far as I can see, nothing much is going to happen until tomorrow,' Dobbie replied.

Dobbie and Handley had been friends for some time and often played together on Sunday mornings. Like Dobbie, Handley lived on his own, his wife having finally refused to put up any longer with his excessive drinking. He was now divorced. This had come about when he was a flat-race trainer in Berkshire. Trying to continue on his own had not been a success and after struggling for a few years, with the number of owners and horses under his care steadily diminishing, he had handed in his licence and moved to Devon. His livelihood now depended on a small cattle farm and taking in injured racehorses, mainly jumpers, who needed prolonged rest before returning to their trainers.

He was some ten years older than Dobbie and they had met when the latter was also living in Berkshire. At first, Dobbie had taken up the role of the younger man befriended by the fairly well-known trainer, but imperceptibly he had come to play a more dominant part in the friendship.

'I've been doing some thinking and I've come up with a theory,' Handley opined after a while.

'What's that?'

'Alan Oppenheim recently lost Grayling a lot of money.'

'How come?'

'Some marvellous company in Argentina had discovered oil, or thought they had. Alan put Grayling into the shares and then it turned out there wasn't any oil. The shares collapsed to pennies.'

'One of the risks of investing in companies like that, wouldn't you say?'

'Yes, but there was subsequently an article in one of the Sunday papers stating that Alan's stockbroking firm had made plenty of money out of it. They'd acquired a good chunk of the company cheaply before they floated it on the Stock Exchange. There was good support for the shares in the financial columns afterwards, so the price went way up. All I can say is, when the collapse came, Alan and his partners appeared to own no shares.'

'But he hadn't told Grayling to sell?'

'No, and Grayling was threatening to make trouble, was looking around for other people who might be in the same position, who would support him.'

'And if it were proved that Alan had acted dishonestly, even fraudulently, he might find himself "warned off" the Stock Exchange – or whatever they call it there.'

'Yes ... and goodbye to his living.'

Dobbie sank into thought.

'If it *were* Alan who killed Grayling, knowing him I should think he'd have an irreproachable alibi,' he remarked with a laugh.

Neither man spoke. Then Dobbie suddenly said, 'You've got a motive yourself.'

'What on earth do you mean?' Handley spluttered.

'Didn't you sell him a horse a little while ago, which he never paid for?'

'How did you know that?' Starting to get red in the face, Handley went on: 'It's true the trainer of one of the crocks I've got on my place told me the owner didn't want it back and asked me to try and sell it. It appeared to be completely recovered and, as it had some excellent previous form, I suggested to Grayling it might be fun for him to have a racehorse. He agreed to pay what they wanted and we sent it to another trainer I know. Unfortunately it broke down again soon afterwards.'

'And Grayling refused to pay you?'

'Yes. It was very unfair, because I had paid for it earlier and it was leaving me short of cash. Mind you, he probably only wanted it in the first place as a chance of some easy money.'

'So, in theory of course, you could have confronted him on the golf-course and in a fit of temper given him a clout over the head – perhaps with a club snatched from his own bag! Not meaning to kill him, obviously,' Dobbie added hastily.

'And then carried the body into the wood?' Handley cried out sarcastically. Quietening down, he went on softly: 'I'm not a murderer, wouldn't have it in me. You'll have to think of somebody else.'

'David, we're friends. I was only theorising. It's up to the police to solve the crime. I was just trying to show they may find it extremely difficult.'

Ian Dobbie couldn't remember the man's name, but they'd played against each other once in an inter-club competition and swapped telephone numbers afterwards. After searching through his address book, he found what he wanted.

The telephone rang for a long time, but eventually he got an answer.

'Tim Thompson,' a man's voice said.

'Oh Tim,' Ian began. 'Awfully sorry to bother you on a Sunday afternoon. It's Ian Dobbie – don't know if you remember but...'

''Course I remember you. You were the one who sunk me and my partner with that fantastic birdie out of the bunker at the last.'

Ian laughed. 'Look, it's a bit of a cheek ringing up the area Superintendent himself like this, but we've had a spot of bother at the club. In fact, someone's been murdered ... the captain in actual fact.'

'Not Grayling? I remember him too.'

'Yes, I'm afraid so. Found clobbered to death in the rough. The point is our local policeman doesn't seem to be treating the case with all that much urgency. Talking about an Inspector coming in the morning. I think it's really important to get a police doctor, if nobody else, over this afternoon. Say there turns out to be a number of suspects, shouldn't we be establishing the approximate time of death before it becomes more difficult? Alibis and all that sort of thing...'

'Don't worry about an Inspector in the morning, I'll come over myself right away. Good excuse to stop gardening! See you in about an hour.'

'Terribly good of you. But ... a doctor?'

'Is Grayling still where he was found?'

'Yes.'

'Well, leave him there. I'll want to have a look around first, but then we can move him to the clubhouse and I'll make sure some sort of doctor's on hand. If I'm a bit late, you'll know it's because I'm having to do a bit of ringing round.' Then, after a pause, 'I've got a stretcher in the garage – I'll bring that with me.'

Thanking him effusively, Ian put the phone down.

It was a little after six o'clock when Ian was back in the clubhouse. There were a few groups of people sitting having drinks, but the first thing Ian noticed was Lord Ancaster sitting up at the bar chatting to Albert, the steward. He went up to talk to him, but turning round in his seat, Ancaster was the first to speak.

'Decided to come over and check on any developments.'

'Has that policeman been back or anybody from the police rung up?' asked Ian, turning to the steward.

The steward shook his head.

'In that case, nothing very much has happened so far,' Ian remarked to Ancaster. 'But Superintendent Thompson will be here shortly and he's laying on a doctor. In the meantime, we're to leave Grayling where he is.'

'Do all these people know what's happened?' asked Ancaster, waving a hand at the other occupants of the room.

The steward answered. 'I'm afraid the news

got round pretty fast, but as far as I know nobody has made any attempt to, er, view the body.'

Ian climbed on a stool at the bar and ordered a glass of beer. They sat and waited for the Superintendent.

A big, strong man, he shook hands jovially with Ian when he arrived and Ian introduced him to Lord Ancaster.

'I and my partner found the body,' Ian explained, 'and Lord Ancaster, who was following us, then came to have a look. As far as we know, nobody else has been near.'

'All right, you can take me to the scene,' Thompson said to Ian.

'Did you touch anything when you found Grayling?' Thompson asked, as he and Ian set off towards the fairway where Dobbie and David had been playing.

'I turned him over to establish cause of death.'

The Superintendent did not reply.

They made their way through the undergrowth to the copse where the body lay.

'Quite a little path,' Thompson observed.

'That would be me and my partner, then me and Ancaster, then me and the policeman. When I first went in with my partner, it was thick jungle.

'What made you go in in the first place?'

'My partner lost his ball, sent in his Labrador

to find it, then when he wouldn't come out, we blundered our way through to where we heard him crying.'

When they came to where the murdered man was lying, Thompson bent over the body. 'Sharp blow to the side of the head,' he murmured. 'Could have been done by a golf-club. Where *are* his golf-clubs, incidentally? Presumably he was having a round when this happened.'

They spent several minutes searching, but to no avail. 'Doesn't matter,' the Superintendent said, 'I'll have a team of men here in the morning combing the whole area. I think we'll go back and get that stretcher.'

They went straight to Thompson's car, then, leaving the stretcher outside the main door, walked into the clubhouse. All the other members had gone, except for Ancaster, who was still talking with the steward at the bar. Beside them stood a tall man, not unlike the Superintendent in build, but older. Thompson introduced him to Dobbie and Ancaster as Dr Carter. Ian recognised the name as that of a local doctor.

'Can you hang on for a while?' Thompson said to the doctor. 'We're just going to get the body. And can you two please help Dobbie and me,' he went on, turning to the two at the bar, 'by walking over towards the thirteenth fairway in a few minutes, in case we need a relief party half-way back?'

Ian couldn't help but think of the incongruity

206

of the steward and a peer of the realm acting as stretcher bearers.

The Superintendent was a big man and picked up Grayling's body without difficulty, placing it on the stretcher. He and Dobbie then got hold of the stretcher at each end. They met the other two on the way back, but as they were going easily enough did not avail themselves of their services.

'Where can we put him so the doctor can examine him?' Thompson asked the steward when they reached the clubhouse.

At length it was agreed to place the body on the large table in the committee room. Ian found himself imagining what some of the committee members might have thought.

While they were waiting for the doctor to carry out his task, the local policeman appeared, carrying a sheet and ropes and several stakes.

The policeman started stammering when the Superintendent introduced himself.

'Don't worry, you did all you could,' Thompson assured him. 'I happened to hear about it personally and decided to get things moving. You won't need the sheet, but no harm in roping off the area from the edge of the fairway side. I don't want any more people going in there. Can you find your way back on your own?'

Nodding, the constable replied, 'I think so, sir.'

'All right then.' Turning to the steward, Thompson said, 'My men will be coming in the morning to check the surroundings. That hole must be closed for play tomorrow and nobody is to go in the rough on the right. I rely on you to put up prominent notices here and in the locker room. Is that understood?'

'We don't get many people on a Monday,' the steward answered, 'and I'll see there's somebody on the first tee to make sure they've all understood.'

'Can I say a word please, sir?' asked the constable, addressing the Superintendent.

'Yes, what is it?'

'I understand the deceased is named Grayling. This morning a Mrs Grayling rang the station to report her husband missing.'

'A bit late, wasn't it, if it turns out her husband was killed yesterday or even earlier?'

'All she told me was her husband was in the habit of staying out overnight sometimes, but he always warned her. She didn't think he had done so this time, but she couldn't remember for sure.'

'What did you do about it?'

'I telephoned Exeter for him to be listed as a missing person, sir.'

'Does that mean she has not been told about this tragedy?' the Superintendent remarked to no one in particular.

Dr Carter had reappeared, having overheard the conversation. 'The lady is a patient of mine,' he broke in. 'She was stricken with multiple sclerosis some years ago and has been confined

208

to a wheelchair for the last few months. Sadly, in addition, her memory has started to deteriorate. It would be difficult to establish whether her husband had warned her or not.'

The Superintendent grunted. 'Well, what conclusion have you come to?'

'Cause of death is as you will have seen. *Time* of death would be sometime in the last forty eight hours. I am sorry I cannot be more precise. I should like to suggest the body be taken by ambulance to the hospital and that one of your regular police doctors, when available, carries out a detailed examination in more appropriate surroundings.

'Now, if you will excuse me, I feel it is my duty to go and see Mrs Grayling, to break the news, or, if she already knows, at any rate to commiserate.'

The doctor departed, after shaking hands with the Superintendent and nodding to the others. The steward took it upon himself to observe that Mr Grayling was in the habit of playing nine holes on his own of a Saturday evening. Thompson asked where the telephone was, in order to arrange for an ambulance and also apprise the main station at Exeter of the developments since the local policeman's telephone call.

When he returned, he started asking Ian and Ancaster about the geography of the course. What was behind that copse where the body was found? Could it be approached from another way? Would it be possible to get a car near it? How far did the club's land go back?

The two men's vague answers did not satisfy him. The steward, who might have known, had taken himself off somewhere. Ian offered to go and look for him, but Thompson waved the idea aside. 'My team will give me all the answers I want tomorrow,' he said.

When he had gone, Ancaster took Ian aside. 'Something I want to tell you,' he said quietly. 'Let's go and sit on the terrace.'

They chose a table at the far end, although there was nobody else there. 'I used to be on the committee, as you may know,' Ancaster began, 'and I was quite friendly with Grayling, not that I ever liked him, I have to say. Anyhow, a week or so ago – I suppose he wanted someone to confide in – he told me he was pretty sure Albert, our steward, was helping himself to a lot of the bar takings. Grayling couldn't understand why they had dropped so much. Also, he started testing whether Albert was putting green fees through the books. You know that whenever the pro's shop is closed for any reason, the custom is visitors settle for them at the bar. Well, he was pocketing them. Grayling had it out with him and there was an almighty row...'

'Oh my God,' Ian exploded, 'we don't want any more suspects!'

'What d'you mean?'

'Nothing! What's the position with Albert? Did Grayling give him the sack?'

'That is something I don't know. I never saw him again before he was killed.'

Edward Grayling had been not only the captain of the club and chairman of the committee but the unpaid secretary as well, a job he had offered to take on, with the committee's agreement, when the previous secretary had retired early in the summer. It had been generally assumed that he found his home life depressing, in the company of his sick wife and the woman who looked after her, and relished the excuse to spend extra time at the club. He was responsible for keeping the books, arranging the catering with the cook and generally overseeing the staff, both in the clubhouse and outside. Apart from anything else, who was going to run the club now, Ian wondered?

Saying goodbye to a departing Ancaster, Ian wandered into the locker room. He knew where the captain's locker was, but it would probably be locked. Still, no harm in checking. He was giving his role of self-appointed detective full rein. The locker door was slightly open. Inside was a golf-bag, crammed with clubs. He grabbed a paper towel and went through the clubs. Yes, there was one missing: a seven iron. Could that be the club that had dealt the fatal blow? And why hadn't the murderer cleaned it and put it back? Perhaps there had not been time. Hardly looked as if Grayling had been killed during his quiet round of evening golf though, if he hadn't taken his clubs.

Ian was giving himself a late breakfast on the following morning when he heard his name called from the hall.

'Ian, are you there?'

It was Daphne's husband, the retired Wing Commander.

He came into the kitchen. 'Daphne told me you'd called round. Didn't dare come and see you last night – I was in such a rage.'

'Look, Tommy, I wasn't accusing you of anything. Just wanted you to be on your guard.'

'Well, it was preposterous to suppose I could have had anything to do with Edward's murder.'

Ian poured him out a cup of tea.

'Do you think he was attacked while he was out playing on the course?'

'Personally, no. But the police are on to it all. A search of the area where he was found is being made – they're probably at it now.'

'Edward certainly behaved very badly towards me. I never understood the reason, but he seemed determined I should not be allowed to become a member.'

'No idea why?'

212

'No idea whatsoever.'

Ian wondered whether the man was speaking the truth.

'Do you know that one of the reasons I bought my house was that it was so near the club? I was looking forward to playing on the course several times a week. As it is, I'm obliged to pay a green fee every time I play. And I can tell you that that mounts up, so I don't play that often – I can't afford to. I've only got my pension to live on, you know.'

'D'you reckon that with Edward out of the way you'll now have a better chance of being elected?'

'I'll certainly have a go.'

Ian looked at the broad, squat figure sitting at the other side of the table. Tough, not lacking in charm, he had spent most of his time in the RAF on active service overseas.

The Wing Commander had not been long gone when Lord Ancaster and two members of the committee, whom Ian knew slightly, called to see him. Hesitatingly, they asked him if he would agree to take on the job of honorary secretary of the club. Only temporarily, of course, but they needed someone with the time and the common sense they knew he possessed. They were sure the appointment would be welcomed by both members and staff.

Ian had not been expecting the approach, but was not particularly surprised by it. Immersed as he had become in the murder and his eagerness to solve it, he quickly realised that the position he was being offered might easily afford him opportunities otherwise difficult to pursue. He accepted readily, to the relief of his callers.

He decided that his first priority would be to go and see Edward Grayling's widow. As the new secretary, it was surely appropriate to pay an early afternoon call and offer the sympathy and condolences of the club's members.

The door of the house was opened by an elderly woman, who, when he explained who he was and the purpose of his visit, asked him to wait in the hall. Shortly after, he was shown into a small sitting-room to be confronted by a lady sitting in a wheelchair, with a rug over her knees down to her ankles, who held out a hand for him to shake. She motioned him to an upright chair nearby and asked the other woman, hovering in the doorway, to bring them some tea.

'What a terrible business,' Ian said softly, after finishing his formal remarks.

'The Superintendent came to see me an hour ago,' replied Mrs Grayling. 'I told him I can't think who could have done it. Was there really someone who hated him so much?'

She spoke clearly and firmly. Her unfortunate condition had certainly not affected her voice. She looked younger than Ian had supposed; probably in her early fifties, and, although her face was now lined, it was clear she had once been attractive.

'Of course, the blow is even worse for me, handicapped like this. I relied on Edward in so many ways. Fortunately I have Laura. She comes in every day to look after me and get my meals. I can still get myself in and out of bed, and wheel myself around the ground floor, but that is about all.'

'No walking?'

'I'm afraid that is beyond me now – even with a frame.'

'You have a nice doctor – I met him for the first time yesterday.'

'Yes, he is very kind. He keeps a good eye on me!'

Ian drank a second cup of tea and departed, promising to call again.

Again as the new secretary, he rang Albert on his mobile phone to tell him he would shortly be appearing, and motored to the club. His life had certainly been busy enough since David Handley's tee-shot into the rough the previous morning, he thought. The clock was striking five as he arrived, to be told that Superintendent Thompson had just been enquiring for him on the phone. Ian noticed, along with prominent announcements about the thirteenth hole being closed, one about himself and his new appointment.

'Did the Superintendent let loose all his sleuths in the wilds this morning?' he asked Albert.

215

'There appeared quite a number of them, sir.'

'Did they find any clues?'

'I don't know, sir. After about two hours, they were all back in the car-park and drove off in their vehicles.' Then, handing Ian a piece of paper, the steward added, 'The Superintendent said would you ring him back on this number, sir?'

Ian went to the room that had always been the secretary's office and which would now be his own domain. There was a key in the door, which he put in his pocket. Although the door was not locked, the room did not appear to have been searched by the police or anybody else for that matter. Looking in cupboards and drawers, everything was undisturbed. There were small piles of papers on the desk itself, doubtless items awaiting Grayling's attention. Still, now that he had been appointed to his official position, Ian intended to make sure the room remained private.

'Didn't come up with much this morning,' Thompson said, after Ian got through. He was speaking from his office. 'I'm looking to you to help me all you can, incidentally, especially as you've now become secretary! Congratulations!'

'News certainly travels fast,' laughed Ian. 'What did your people find out about access from the rear of that wood?'

'Easy enough, and with a car too. It's farmland beyond, but there's a track from the main road. And another thing that will interest you – they didn't find any golf-clubs.'

Ian decided to make no mention at this point of having found them in Grayling's locker.

'I'm in Grayling's office now,' he said, 'and tomorrow I'm going to search through everything. Will let you know how I get on.'

'Was hoping you'd say that,' Thompson replied. 'Frankly, you're more likely to spot something relevant than one of my officers. At the same time, leave any interviewing of suspects to us!'

Ian locked the door on his way out.

'Has anyone been into Mr Grayling's old office today, Albert?' Ian asked the steward as he was leaving.

'No, sir. It's been locked ever since Mr Grayling last used it. I expect he had the key on him when he died. I keep a duplicate key here in case of fire and I unlocked the door and left it in the keyhole when you rang to say you were coming.'

Ian was back in Edward Grayling's office at eight o'clock on the following morning. It was Tuesday. He extracted a bulky file labelled 'members' from a cupboard. It consisted of records of subscription payments. He was about to put it back when he noticed some letters clipped together, stuffed into the back of the file. He took them out and sat down at the desk.

The correspondence was between Wing Commander Tommy Byecroft and Grayling. Byecroft's letters were hand written, while

Grayling's were carbon copies of ones he had written on an old typewriter. Fascinated, Ian slowly read through them. They were all about a girl, a young girl it seemed, who was the daughter of an aircraftman who had once served under Byecroft. The aircraftman apparently lived locally and had complained to his senior officer from service days of an alleged indecent assault on the girl by none other than Grayling. The correspondence was short and ended at a date some two years before, with Grayling threatening to take Byecroft to court for unfounded and malicious libel, should he hear from him again. He refused to be confronted by either the girl or her father.

Ian wondered whether there was any truth behind the charge. He found it difficult to imagine Grayling making an indecent assault on anyone. He might have been drunk, he supposed. The late club captain was known to be fond of his pink gins. Even so, the accusation hardly fitted with Ian's own idea of Grayling's character. He put the letters back in the file; it would be up to the police to take the matter up with the Wing Commander in due course ... and find and interview the aircraftman. Still, if the aircraftman *were* the murderer, he had taken a long time to get around to it.

Ian found the club's bank statements in another file. The credit columns showed in the main the members' renewal subscriptions. There were numerous entries on the debit side, payments – he supposed – to various suppliers, together with the monthly payments, by bank transfer, to the full-time indoor and outdoor staff. But ... in the previous six months there had been three large withdrawals to cash, one for £2,000 and two for £1,000. What had those been for? The club had very limited cash requirements. In fact, all Ian could think of were the cash payments to the one or two boys who came to help the ground-staff in the summer months. The professional had his own arrangements, paying the club an annual fee and keeping the money earned from giving lessons and the profit on goods he sold in his shop. It was his responsibility to pay for new stock. Ian went back through the statements for several years and could find no similar withdrawals.

He was interrupted by Albert, the steward, coming in with a tray. 'Thought you might like a cup of coffee, sir,' he said.

'Thank you. Put it down. Now, as you're here, can you give me any reason why Mr Grayling should have needed to have withdrawn four thousand pounds from the bank in cash over the last few months?'

'Awkward for me to say, sir.'

'How do you mean? Do you know of a reason or not?'

Albert continued to look evasive. At length he said, 'Perhaps he was having personal financial problems, sir.'

'Like being blackmailed, for instance?'

'I couldn't say, sir.'

Ian saw he was not going to get any information out of the steward at this point and changed the line of attack.

'Albert, I gather you were recently in a spot of trouble with Mr Grayling. He alleged you were pocketing money in your position at the bar, instead of putting it through the books.'

'Yes, sir, I admitted it and promised to pay it back.'

'Did Mr Grayling give you your notice?'

'No, sir. He let me off with a warning.'

'Would you say there was any special reason for his being so lenient? Like your knowing something about him, which he would not want made public?'

'No, sir.'

'All right, Albert, you may go. And if by any chance Wing Commander Byecroft is in the club today, would you tell him I should like to see him?'

'He paid his green fee and set off for a round on his own about an hour ago. I'll tell him when he comes in.'

'Happened to stumble on some correspondence between you and Grayling earlier this morning,' said Ian, when Byecroft appeared in the office some two hours later. Ian had spent the interim sorting out the papers on the top of Grayling's desk and going through the contents of the drawers. Everything was concerned with run-of-the-mill club matters and he had found no more surprises.

'I was in a difficult situation,' Byecroft began. 'This man, who used to be under my command, was putting me under a lot of pressure to help him ... was convinced the girl's allegations were true.'

'Why couldn't he and the daughter have gone and had it out with Grayling on their own?'

'They'd already tried. They called at his house one evening, but he threw them out. Said he didn't know what they were talking about, said it was completely unfounded.'

'They should have gone to the police, if the girl was so sure.'

Byecroft hesitated. 'I found out later she'd made a complaint of this nature before, about some other man,' he said, 'which they'd dismissed. Look, she knew Edward all right. She worked here in the kitchen for a time. Described how it had happened one afternoon in his office.'

'I think it was a great pity you let yourself get involved. There's no doubt you antagonised Edward. Was it at a time your name was down for membership?'

'Unfortunately, yes.'

'Well, the correspondence I found is now two years old. What happened in the end?'

'I persuaded them both to drop it. Gave them a bit of money, of course.'

'Didn't think you had any money. You told me you'd only got your pension.'

'I'd rather not go into this any more, if you don't mind,' Byecroft said bluntly. 'It obviously has nothing to do with Edward's death. And now, with his death, the whole thing's a closed book.'

'I think the police might still want to question your aircraftman, find out where he was on the day or night in question. Did you apologise to Edward, incidentally?'

'I tried to, but he was too incensed, wouldn't accept it. He went out of his way to ignore me ever after.'

If Grayling were innocent, Ian doubted he was the kind of man to steal money from the club just to get rid of a nuisance. And the money had been withdrawn so long after the incident was meant to have happened. There must be another connection, Ian thought. Was he gambling? Yes, gambling on the Stock Exchange, certainly! Ian recalled what David Handley had told him of Grayling's anger over the failed investment he had made through Alan Oppenheim. He would arrange to have a talk with Mr Oppenheim.

Meanwhile, who were the more immediate suspects? Handley had got a motive, but was unlikely to have had the courage to do the deed

– unless, of course, it was not premeditated. Albert did not seem to have a motive, particularly as the captain had not given him the sack, although he had been less than open with Ian that morning. Tommy Byecroft? Nothing to gain, except perhaps at last being permitted to become a member. The aircraftman would have had to have been smouldering for a very long time; Byecroft had not suggested that the girl had subsequently become ill through shock or had a baby. However, it might be natural for an outsider, with no knowledge of the club, to dump the body in a wild part of the golf-course grounds, imagining its discovery less likely on private land that nobody would go near.

Conversely, if the murderer *did* have knowledge of the club, he might still put the body in the copse, Ian ruminated. But he would plan to come back later and bury it. He would be all too aware of certain members' habits of bringing their dogs out. Discovery of an unburied corpse would be only a matter of time. Unfortunately, discovery had come too soon.

One thing appeared certain: outsider or insider, the murder had occurred elsewhere and the body had been taken to the spot by car up the track at the back of the wood.

Byecroft was sitting in the bar, having a pint of beer, as Ian left the club to go to his car. He made a call to Daphne Byecroft on his mobile phone and asked her to meet him at his house as soon as possible. She was already there, outside in her car, when he arrived.

'Thought I'd leave while Tommy was still out,' she said, smiling. 'Didn't want him asking me where I was going.'

They went inside and Ian offered to make some coffee. In the end, they decided on opening a bottle of white wine.

'Just had a bit of an altercation with your husband,' Ian said. 'Do you know anything about some man who served under Tommy in the RAF and alleges Edward Grayling assaulted his daughter?'

'Edward?' cried Daphne. 'Can't think of anybody less likely!'

She knew absolutely nothing about the matter.

'Well, please don't say anything to Tommy about my having told you. According to him, this man brought him in to try and get his help.'

'How did the girl know it was Edward?'

'She used to work at the club, evidently. But the story could easily be fabricated.'

After a long sip from her glass, Daphne said, 'It's all part of his quick temper – Tommy can get unreasonably obsessed over things. I suppose he started taxing Edward about it? It was nothing to do with him.'

'I'm not saying anything to the police anyway, until I'm satisfied it's material,' Ian said.

224

They were both still standing, and Daphne, putting down her glass, suddenly threw her arms around his neck. 'Thank you for not making my life even more difficult,' she whispered. Ian held her tightly, his cheek against hers. Why was her life so difficult?

Ian had made a note of Oppenheim's home phone number from records at the club and that evening he rang him at his house in London.

'I expect you've heard about Grayling's murder,' he said. 'I've been appointed temporary secretary and I'm helping the Superintendent down here with what they call enquiries.'

'Yes, David Handley phoned on Sunday evening and told me,' Oppenheim broke in. 'I had to stay in London last weekend, so knew nothing about it. Terrible news. I wish I could help you.'

'Perhaps you can.'

'I don't see how. I was nowhere near the place last weekend.'

'All the same, I'd appreciate having a talk with you.'

'What about exactly?'

'Well, to come straight to the point, I understand Grayling was in a bit of a state about an investment you'd made for him.'

There was silence at the other end of the line.

'Could you see me if you're down next weekend?' Ian went on.

'The sooner I explain all about that to you the better,' Oppenheim at last remarked. 'Have you got any engagement tomorrow night?'

'No.'

'In that case, I'll motor down after work and see you at your house.'

'I'll look forward to it,' said Ian. 'I'll be there waiting for you.'

He had just put the phone down, when it started to ring. It was Superintendent Thompson.

'Was at the club this afternoon,' he said. 'Albert told me you'd been in earlier. We're still looking for the murder weapon. My forensic people seem pretty sure it was a golf-club. Anyway, I got Albert to open all the lockers with his master key…'

'I was going to tell you,' interrupted Ian, 'I found Grayling's clubs in his locker.'

'Yes, I rather assumed they might be there, as we didn't find them near the body. We started off with that locker, and there was one club missing – a seven iron.'

Ian said nothing. After a pause, the Superintendent continued: 'I told Albert he needn't wait and I carefully looked through all the other lockers. I was about half-way through when I found a bag with two number sevens in it. I took the one that didn't match the set in the locker and compared it with Grayling's clubs. It was an exact match.

'I left Albert shutting up all the lockers again and took the club back to Exeter with me, to get it fingerprinted and examined for blood stains.'

'But could you see whose locker it was where you found it?'

'Yes, unlike some of them, it had a name on the door.'

'I suppose the murderer could have put it in a completely innocent person's locker,' observed Ian.

'If it happened to be unlocked,' replied the Superintendent. 'But that's why I'm not making an arrest at the moment.'

On the next morning, Wednesday, Albert started to tell Ian about the Superintendent's visit. He took away a golf-club, he informed Ian, but the steward didn't know in which locker he had found it. There were no members within earshot and Ian decided to get the man talking about Edward Grayling again. 'You were saying yesterday you thought Mr Grayling might have had money worries,' he said.

'Sometimes he seemed very depressed,' the steward answered, in a more forthcoming manner than during their previous interview. 'I put it down to his wife's illness, but it could have been money. He was certainly more sympathetic than I expected ... when he found me out and I told him about *my* money troubles.'

'Would you describe him as a ladies' man?'

'How do you mean, sir?'

'Well, did you ever hear of any scandal or ever see any lady friends?'

'I certainly never heard of any scandal, sir, although we had to get rid of a kitchen girl here once, who was trying to get him interested in her. It was laughable, if it hadn't been so embarrassing.'

'What about lady friends?'

'Oh, at one time there were a few of those around,' the steward chuckled. 'Came and collected him in their cars sometimes. I used to think – still waters run deep. But that was all a little while ago now.'

'Thank you, Albert,' Ian said. Then, seeing a perplexed look come over the man's face, he added:

'I'm just trying to get to the bottom of this business – that's all.'

At about eight o'clock that evening, Alan Oppenheim appeared, as arranged, at Ian's house. He had had something to eat on the way down and declined the offer of a drink.

In his mid-forties, short, swarthy, he sat down and peered at Ian through tinted glasses.

'I used to play with Edward sometimes, as you probably know,' he started slowly. 'I found him a strange man in many ways. For a retired solicitor, I didn't get the impression he had much money. He was always asking me to look out for a money-making opportunity on the Stock Exchange. Well, something came up – an oil and gas exploration company in Argentina. My firm was approached to raise development capital for them and we agreed, but it was highly speculative – a fact that we of course stressed in the prospectus.'

'Nevertheless, you and your partners acquired a large holding in the company before you offered the stock to the public, I believe?' Ian queried, repeating what David Handley had told him.

'I suppose you read that article in the Sunday paper,' Oppenheim replied glumly. Then, without elaboration, 'We're suing them. Anyway, Edward, instead of having a little punt, insisted on going in rather heavily. Some other paper had talked about investors possibly making five or ten times their money, which was ridiculous in the short term...'

'And I gather he lost the lot,' put in Ian.

'Yes, I'm afraid so. The market got wind that their main well wasn't performing and the shares plummeted.'

'The Sunday paper said, I gather, that you and your partners got out in time. That must have upset him.'

'Yes, it was very unfortunate. There wasn't time to get him and some of the other clients out.'

'How did you all manage it?'

'We had what's known as a stop loss on our shares. When they started to fall, our shares were automatically sold in the market, at a prescribed price, without any reference.'

'But the clients' shares didn't have a stop loss?'

'No. And things moved so quickly, there wasn't time to get their instructions.'

'Well, it's not for me to comment on your ethics,' Ian remarked cheerfully. 'Please understand I'm only trying to help the Superintendent in charge of this unfortunate case.'

'He could hardly feel that I had anything to do with the murder...'

'I expect not. But a member here told me Edward was trying to make trouble for you.'

Oppenheim looked surprised. 'I didn't know he was talking about it in the club. You go into a speculative share and sometimes you lose your shirt. It's as simple as that.'

'I think what rankled was you and your partners had got out.'

'I have to admit he wrote to the Stock Exchange Council, complaining.'

'Might you be in trouble with them?'

'These things take a long time. They're always getting complaints about something or other. They interviewed me and my senior partner. But I don't think it will come to anything. We may get censured for failing to recommend clients took out stop losses, that is all.'

'And why didn't you?'

'The market wouldn't have been strong enough to have stood too large a quantity and the exercise would have become academic.'

Ian had not really understood Oppenheim's last remark, but decided to enquire no further. Delving into Stock Exchange practices and business methods of a particular broking firm were outside what he was seeking to achieve. He had no way of knowing if Oppenheim's assertion that he was unlikely to be in serious trouble was true or not. If it were untrue, he supposed Oppenheim would have a motive.

'So, even if Edward were still alive, you don't think he could have caused you to become – er – barred?'

'How do you mean?'

'Barred from trading ... from continuing your career on the Exchange.'

'Good Lord, no!' laughed Oppenheim, quickly looking serious again. 'I regret the whole incident most sincerely, of course, and I'm shocked by Edward's death, but I have not broken any Stock Exchange rules as such.'

You may not have done, old boy, thought Ian to himself, but I bet *you* managed to make a nice bit of money along the way. He had never much liked Alan Oppenheim and had now formed an even lower opinion. Still, he was a guest in Ian's house, niceties had to be preserved. He offered the man a drink again, which this time was accepted, and they started to talk about other things.

It was after ten o'clock when the phone rang. Oppenheim had long gone. An excited Daphne was on the line.

'You'll never believe this,' she said, 'I've just seen Mrs Grayling go out to post a letter!'

'OK, what's so extraordinary about that? She can probably just about get out of the house in her wheelchair.'

'She wasn't in her wheelchair.'

There was a silence while Ian collected his thoughts. 'It's dark, how do you know it was her? Probably the carer.'

'It was her all right. There's a bright moon tonight and I saw her face.'

'Did she see you?'

'I don't think so. You know her house is on a little green, which has a post-box on it? I was in my car, coming back from a charity meeting, and I'd slowed down to go round the corner, and she was there, walking towards the box!'

'Thanks for telling me,' said Ian. 'It's certainly strange. I went to see her the other day, as it happens, and she told me quite definitely she was unable to walk.'

'What are you going to do?' asked Daphne.

'Let me think about it.' Ian paused, then said, 'How are you? Is everything all right at home? I've been thinking of you ... the way you said your life was difficult.'

'I'm all right. But looking forward to seeing you again!'

Thursday morning found Ian Dobbie sitting

opposite Mrs Grayling in her sitting-room, sipping a cup of coffee.

'I don't know what Superintendent Thompson would think of my coming to see you like this,' he began, when the carer had left them and the door was shut. '*He's* the one who's in charge of the investigation into Edward's murder...'

Mrs Grayling looked at him blankly.

'Why, have you found anything out, which you don't yet want to talk to him about?' she asked kindly.

'Yes, I have. And I'm afraid it concerns you.'

'So Daphne Byecroft has spoken to you. I recognised her when she went by in her car. We used to see each other quite often at one time – decorating the church, good works, that sort of thing.'

Ian took another drink from his cup of coffee and said nothing.

'Edward had been, shall I say, a disappointment to me for some time. I knew about his girlfriends and that girl at the club...'

'You knew about her?' Ian interrupted.

'Yes, that was complete nonsense, of course. But, more to the point, he had started stealing *my* money. He'd managed to get through all of his own – on his girlfriends, for all I know. He tried to hide my bank statements from me, but one day the bank rang me up to tell me I was overdrawn!'

'You have an income of your own then?'

'Yes, dividends from shares I bought when my father died and I sold his house. I suppose the last straw was when I found out that he had forged my signature and actually sold some of the shares themselves. All right, I'm still probably only in the early stages of this disease – not quite so crocked as I make out to Dr Carter – but I'm going to get worse rather than better and I'll need money to see me through. I couldn't let it go on.'

Mrs Grayling paused for breath. She had become slightly agitated by what she had said.

A good minute passed, then Ian said, 'So you started thinking of a plan to be rid of him?'

'Yes. I had been diagnosed a few years ago now and I decided to make out I was quickly getting worse. Said I couldn't walk any more, had to have a person to look after me, and even pretended my mind was going.'

'So nobody could suspect you?'

There was no answer.

'But, in the meantime, he could have been taking more of your money?'

'I didn't worry about that, as long as he was paying for the carer and the household bills. All I wanted was to protect the capital and I told the bank to send me the share certificates they were holding, and I hid them here. That way he could be selling away happily, but no sale would ever be effected, because he wouldn't have access to the certificates.'

'Didn't he ever ask you where they were?'

'Yes, he did once, and I told him our daughter was holding them. They didn't get on well, so he wouldn't have got much change out of her.'

'So, if you'd secured your financial future, why did you have to take such a drastic step?'

'Do you mean killing him? I hated him,' she said matter-of-factly, 'and the other night, after he'd been particularly beastly, I waited till he was asleep and went into his bedroom and hit him with all my might.'

'On the left temple?'

'I don't know which temple, but he was sleeping on his side.'

Ian's coffee had gone cold, but he finished it up. 'I suppose you're making a mistake in telling me all this,' he said.

'Because I'll go to prison? It won't be much worse than my life at present. Besides, it's a relief getting everything off my chest. The mental strain has been as bad as my illness.'

'One thing – who were you posting the letter to?'

'A very dear friend. We don't like being seen together too often. But we correspond.'

'And would it be that dear friend who disposed of the body for you?'

Mrs Grayling did not reply.

'Did Edward never see your post?' Ian went on.

'It comes late every morning. He'd always left for the golf club.'

235

Ian got up to go. 'I'll leave it to you to repeat all this to the Superintendent,' he said.

'Aren't you going to ask to see the murder weapon?' Mrs Grayling enquired, with the hint of a smile. She got up from her wheelchair abruptly and told him to follow her. Walking steadily but slowly, she led him into the cloakroom off the hallway.

Ian thought he was the ultimate in golf enthusiasts and in acquiring every other new club that came on the market, but he realised he was mistaken when he saw the array of bags and clubs along the walls.

'It was this one,' Mrs Grayling said, and she was actually laughing as she pulled out an iron club from a very old golf-bag.

He had said his goodbyes and Mrs Grayling was back in her wheelchair, when, going out the front door, he met Lord Ancaster coming up the front path.

'Poor old Grayling's widow,' Ancaster muttered. 'Known her as long as I've known Grayling. Just coming to make sure she's all right.'

Ian rang a certain telephone number late that Thursday afternoon. He was told the person he wanted to speak to was out for his usual evening walk.

'I can't remember – where does he usually go?' Ian asked conversationally.

'Oh, along the cliff, starting from Lynmouth. It should be lovely on an evening like this.'

Ian got into his car and in half an hour he was parking in a lay-by at the top of the hill above Lynmouth. He climbed over some wire, crossed a field full of sheep, and was soon on the coastal path. The track was on the edge of a steep cliff, winding for miles, and he looked down on the blue, raging sea, thundering over the rocks at the bottom. He could see nobody to his left, and turned right, away from the town. Before him the track stretched on endlessly. Two holiday-makers, rucksacks over their shoulders, came into view. He made way for them to pass as they wished him good-evening. Then he saw in the distance a tall, broad-shouldered man striding out towards him.

'Good-evening,' said Ian, as the man came abreast. 'You may remember we met a few days ago.'

'I'm afraid you have me there,' came the affable reply. 'Where was it?'

'Superintendent Thompson brought you to our golf club to examine our murdered captain. I had helped bring the body in from where it was found.'

'Of course, of course,' said Dr Carter, shaking hands. 'Silly of me not to remember. Has Thompson come up with any clues yet?'

'Nothing to speak of, as far as I know, but I think I myself have.'

'Ah! Doing a bit of amateur sleuthing, eh?'

'I don't know about sleuthing, but Mrs Grayling has told me certain things,' said Ian slowly.

'Yes? What was that? Been a patient of mine for a long time now.'

'To be blunt, she told me she'd killed her husband. With a golf-club...'

'Good Lord! How terrible! But how could she have done it from her wheelchair?'

'She could walk around all right. Killed him in his sleep. Must have been fooling you all this time.'

'But the body was found on the golf course – or rather in the rough.'

'Yes. A close friend of hers must have moved it.'

'Who on earth could that have been?'

'Perhaps someone who'd known her and loved her for a long time. Someone who remembered how she used to be before the disease struck her. Someone who knew what a hell Edward Grayling was making of her life.'

Dr Carter looked at Ian in a grieved but tolerant way. 'You should be aware that the lady's mind is anything but sound,' he said. 'I'm afraid neither her alleged confession nor your assumptions would be admitted as serious evidence.'

Ian continued on doggedly, regardless of the interruption. 'Then it struck me, Dr Carter, that perhaps you were that someone, that she hadn't been fooling you after all, that you knew about

238

her deception ... about pretending to be virtually paralysed. All done with one aim in view...'

'If you're suggesting that I acted unprofessionally...'

'I'm suggesting more than that, Dr Carter. I'm suggesting that after Mrs Grayling killed her husband in his bed, you removed the body and put it in the wood. Aiding and abetting, if you like.'

'I hope you haven't been telling the Superintendent about these wild ideas of yours,' the doctor said with a laugh.

'No, I've told nobody ... yet.'

Dr Carter had moved slightly to the inside of the narrow track. Suddenly he grasped Ian below the shoulders, and, lifting him up, made to throw him over the cliff. He was every bit as tall as Ian and for a moment they struggled. Then, managing to get his feet back on the ground, Ian got his leg behind the doctor's knee and screwed him round. As his opponent lost balance, Ian shook himself free and gave an almightly shove. Dr Carter was tottering at the cliff edge when Ian's right foot shot out towards his groin.

Ian could not bring himself to look down the near-perpendicular slope until the doctor's cries had ceased. When he peered over the edge, he saw nothing but the enormous waves.

He walked back to his car. Dark clouds were helping bring about the end of day. There were

no other walkers to be seen. He drove slowly to
Tommy and Daphne Byecroft's house. Tommy
answered the door.

'Come in,' he said. 'Your friend David Handley
is here too.'

Ian smiled to them all and sat down. He
suddenly felt very weak.

'And what's the great detective been able to
find out?' said Tommy, looking at Ian.

'The wife did it.'

He gave them a brief account of all that had
occurred that day. His listeners were horrified.

'And do you know that if it hadn't been for
Daphne nobody would have solved the crime?'

'How do you mean?' said David.

'It was she who told me Mrs Grayling could
still walk. I came here to thank her.'

After a little while, Ian said, 'I'm going to go
home now. I'm not feeling too well.'

Daphne saw him to the door.

'David will be relieved,' she said. 'Edward had
lent him one of his clubs to try out and he
remembered he'd never given it back. But this
afternoon, when he looked, it was no longer in
his golf-bag. Somebody had taken it.'

'Probably the police. But he's got nothing to
worry about now.'

Ian kissed her on the cheek. 'Is your life still
being "difficult"?' he asked.

'Tommy has been head-hunted for a marvellous
job in some small Arab state, reorganising their

Air Force. He's getting bored here and he can certainly do with the money.'

'Will you be going with him?'

'*My* trouble is I can't make up my mind. I don't relish being stuck there for three years.'

'You told me that day we kissed you could never leave Tommy.'

Daphne did not answer.

'Well, if you need me, I'll be around,' said Ian.